KINGS OF
THE NIGHT

WARREN HOLLOWAY

GOOD 2 GO PUBLISHING

KINGS OF THE NIGHT
Written by Warren Holloway
Cover Design: Davida Baldwin, Odd Ball Designs
Typesetter: Mychea
ISBN: 978-1-947340-65-7
Copyright © 2021 Good2Go Publishing
Published 2021 by Good2Go Publishing
7311 W. Glass Lane • Laveen, AZ 85339
www.good2gopublishing.com
https://twitter.com/good2gobooks
G2G@good2gopublishing.com
www.facebook.com/good2gopublishing
www.instagram.com/good2gopublishing

PROLOGUE

"If you're watching this video, please tell my family I love them if they made it. Tell them I'm sorry for what took place. I didn't mean to put them in harm's way," the man in the video said, at the same time breathing heavily and looking over his shoulder as if someone was coming. His eyes zoomed in on the door of what looked like a motel room. "We fucked up bad, I mean really bad. By now you should all know what went wrong. This wasn't supposed to happen. No one knew it was going to go like this." The male in the video stopped speaking, taking hold of the camera and rushing over to the window, peeping out and seeing cars that weren't there before. He also noticed shadows outside of the room, moving around, followed by aggressively speaking voices. Then it happened. The camera phone dropped at the abrupt sound of the motel room door being breached. His eyes shifted to the door in fear. "I'm sorry! Please don't kill me!"

ONE

"TJ, you sure this is the spot with all of the cash?" Chinaman asked.

"Why do you question my Intel? I got an inside man that will benefit from this score," Tony "TJ" Jackson responded. The thirty-four-year-old Afro-American stood six feet even, with a slim build, a close cut that was even all the way around, and a goatee trimmed with precision. He had a military mindset, yet he was always about his money and being punctual, when it counted, like now.

"What do you mean you have someone on the inside? It's already six of us. We don't need someone else entering into this situation that we can't trust," Johnny "Chinaman" Lee stated. The five-foot-nine Asian-American ran his hand through his jet black hair. At the same time, he looked around at the others to see if they agreed with him.

"What we don't need is to split the money with someone else," Richard "Ricky" Washington sta-ted. A proud American with intense blues eyes, he stood six foot two, with a nearly bald head, as if he was fresh out of boot camp. The thirty-six-year-old was also the one most of the team looked up to.

"I'm not sharing my money with anyone," Juan "the Don" Santos said. The thirty-two-year-old

Puerto Rican looking on at his associates with a dark stare assured them that he wouldn't be parting ways with his share of the money. Juan stood six foot even, with black-colored eyes, adding to his distant stare. He had thick eyebrows he tweezed to flow with his slick black hair and a close-shaven beard.

"Everybody calm down," James "Jay" Foster said. "We're not going to lose focus on this very moment. We'll deal with that shit later, but right now, I think that's our guy right there." He pointed at the black male with the duffle bag, walking up the steps to the house they were plotting on. Jay was all business, standing five foot eleven, with a medium build. He had a close cut and brown eyes, and was clean-shaven and well-groomed.

However, tonight they were all wearing black fatigues, lying low behind the tint in the Yukon

Denali XL. The area wasn't saturated with look-outs, like most hoods. This was a little outside of the main strip, where the boss of the B-More streets conducted business.

"Soon as he goes in, we move in on that muthafucka," Chinaman said. "Me and Juan will come through the back, taking them by surprise in case shit gets out of hand."

"Don't worry, Chinaman, we'll do the hard work for you two, which is laying everyone down with no problems."

"Don't get too cocky. That's how men are lost and blood is shed," Ricky said before clambering a round into his AR-15, a statement piece that would get any and everyone's attention upon entering any room. "Let's go get this money so we can all get back to the city and have drink like our ladies think we're doing anyway," he added, taking

4

a deep breath.

As soon as the door closed behind the goon with the duffle bag , the cabin of the truck became quiet as they started pulling the masks down over their faces while readying their weapons for action. Their breathing now shifted as their hearts became full of adrenaline, each of them loving the rush that was coming over them, not knowing what was going to happen once they stormed the house.

TJ hit the gas, accelerating the truck to the front of the house. He came to a halt fast. At the same time, the other five jumped out in sync with trained precision, closing in on the front door. TJ stayed behind the wheel, keeping time while keeping watch. Chinaman rushed to the back with Juan. Jay, Ricky, and Sean "Showtime" Jones, the five-foot-ten green-eyed black male with light skin and wavy hair, "for the ladies," as he would say. Now he was all business so he could get back to the city. Showtime, like the others, met years ago at their previous employer. Since then they'd been bonding like brothers, taking down one goon after another and becoming wealthier each time. To date they'd made over $500,000 in cash and drugs. Tonight the take should be at least four.

There was one hundred thousand in the house. What the inside man didn't know and couldn't tell them was the number of occupants that would be present. Ricky closed in on the door, taking hold of the doorknob and turning it. Nothing. His heart was racing just as fast as his mind, processing his next move. He turned to the others, counting down with three fingers, down to two fingers, down to one. Suddenly, he thrust his foot into the door with brute force, opening it. He rushed in, gun out and aimed at the black male goon still holding the bag they saw him enter with. Showtime and Jay fanned out, taking aim at the four others in the room.

"Don't move, muthafucka, or you won't make it to your next birthday!" Jay shouted as he closed in fast on the goon, reaching for his gun on the side of the end table. He kicked the gun away while giving the goon a dark, murderous look.

"Put the bag down or I'll shoot your arm off until that muthafucka drops!" Ricky said, closing in on the bag and taking hold of it, tossing it over his shoulder. Ricky's eyes scanned the room, not seeing any money visible. At the same time he knew the bag he was holding was heavy and could contain drugs or money.

"Where's the money at, fool?" Jay asked, pointing his gun at the main target on the couch, who was sitting really calmly, as if he was still in control of what was going on. That didn't sit right with them. They could feel it, especially since they came in unexpected with force. That feeling never failed them. As suddenly as those eerie feelings came, they heard someone shouting out.

"Aaagh! Y'all niggas fucked up!" The booming voice shifted all of their attention and weapons, especially after seeing the three hundred-pound thug with a pump-action shotgun chambering a round. The instant spike in adrenaline rushing through their hearts and brains forced them to fear the moment while processing and assessing this situation with lightning speed. Jay took aim with his .45 automatic, finger ready to squeeze the trigger, when a thunderous round sounded off, coming from Chinaman's Glock .44 mm.

The slug slammed with unforgiving force into

the fat goon's head, ejecting his brains and thoughts of bringing harm to the rest of the team. At the same time the other goons tried to take advantage of the moment, seeing the would-be robbers' attention shifting. However, none could move faster than Ricky, Showtime, Jay, China-man, or Juan.

Before Jay could ask for the money, a preteen biracial female started coming down the steps, unaware of the chaos and crime scene unfolding in the living room. She was in town for the week-end with her father. Neither she nor her mother had planned for this type of violence.

Ricky pointed his gun at the young teen, knowing this would expedite the process of getting them what they came for. "Where's the fucking money at, fool?"

"Daddy, please don't let them shoot me!" she

pleaded, frozen in fear, unable to move or flee back up the stairs.

The goon stood from the couch at the same time, staring down Ricky as he pulled back the pillows on the couch, revealing vacuumed-sealed bags of money. "Nobody is going to hurt you, baby girl. Now go back up to your room while Daddy takes care of the bad guys." He waved her up the steps as he came face-to-face with Ricky and his gun, while the others closed in, securing the money. "It's well over four hundred racks. You taking this money is one thing, but my product, too, makes me and everyone in this room a dead man. So before you leave, you better kill me, or we'll find and kill you and everything you love or think about loving," the B-More boss said.

"I look forward to it, but right now, get the fuck on your knees. Secure everyone before we roll out," Ricky said, placing plastic zip ties on the boss just as his team did the others.

"What about the girl?" Jay asked, keeping her in mind.

"Showtime, go secure her," Ricky said as he checked his watch, seeing they'd been in the house longer than planned. Showtime raced up the stairs, sweeping through the rooms before getting to the teen's room.

Immediately his mind went into overdrive, seeing her on her phone looking frantic. He didn't know how long she'd been on the phone or who she was talking to. Could it be the cops? Could it be her mother? He didn't even take the time to find out. He turned quickly, rushing back down the steps. "Let's go right now. She's on the phone."

Hearing him say this, they didn't need to know anything else, because they had been compromised. They all turned, racing out of the house over to the truck and jumping in. As TJ mashed the gas, they could hear the police sirens fast approaching. Not good. This couldn't be happening. They didn't want to get into a shoot-out with the cops, especially being from another city.

"What the fuck happened in there?" TJ asked. "This was supposed to be an in-and-out job."

"There was a full house plus his daughter," Showtime responded. "Plus this fat muthafucka almost got the drop on us, until Chinaman handled that shit like a pro."

"We have to burn this truck and get to the escape vehicle ASAP. We don't know who saw us or heard the gunshots," Chinaman said, removing his mask and placing it into a trash bag with the others. They had already planned to burn the truck and the clothing. As they continued to race through the city of Baltimore, cop cars sped past them, making their way to the house with the traumatized teen crying to the 911 operator.

"This can't happen again. We have to be more precise. No kids, just the muthafuckas with the drugs and money," Juan said, flashing back to the fear in the little girl's eyes. It made him think about his own daughter and little sister. However, in that very moment, having these attachments could not affect the way he moved.

"Juan's right. We have to be more prepared. The fat muthafucka with the shotgun could've easily taken out one or all of us," Ricky said.

"What's done is done, onto the next job. We'll burn this shit and be on our way," TJ said, driving to their getaway vehicles.

Within twenty minutes they were at the getaway vans. They poured alcohol and gasoline inside and out of the truck along with the bag of clothes, before setting it ablaze. Then they jumped into the vans making their escape. They would drive back to Harrisburg, Pennsylvania, their home. They never conducted the nightlife business in their home state—always in other cities, so they could be in and out. As they headed back to the city, they knew this life they lived could never be shared with their wives, girlfriends, and loved ones. In fact, no one outside of their circle would ever know about this. They would kill to keep it a secret. Exposure would mean jail time as well as placing a target on their families and loved ones. This could never happen. They would put their lives on the line to protect all they loved as well as each other.

TWO

TJ and the rest of the team were at the meet-up location, separating the money and the forty kilos they jacked last night. The money, as they all noticed, was more than four hundred stacks. It was more like seven hundred bands, giving each of them a little over a hundred each, plus the breakdown from the bricks when they got rid of them.

"Showtime, you got the hood that can get rid of this work for us, right?" TJ asked.

"Yeah, I got somebody that can get it off, but truth be told, I think we should put the work on hold. You know moving work like this that fast doesn't make sense, plus we're not pressed for the paper right now," he responded before taking a drink of his Mountain Dew MDX energy drink, giving him that morning boost.

"Showtime has a point," Chinaman said. "We keep everything tight, no slipping in any way."

"I'll get a storage unit for a few months, pay it off in advance, so we don't run into any problems," TJ said as he placed the bricks into the bag. At the same time, his burner cell phone sounded off. He removed the phone, seeing that it was Big Black from Baltimore, the six-foot-six 290-pound street thug who gave the inside scoop on the job last night.

TJ answered the phone, "Yo, what's good with you?"

"You know what's good," he responded before continuing on. "That shit is all over the news, plus the streets is talking about that work y'all got."

"Pause on your flow, main man. We don't do the airwaves like that," TJ responded, always being on point even with a burner phone.

"Fuck that shit. You know why I'm hitting you up. So let's get to it. Tell me when we linking up to handle that shit."

"No time soon. I can't come that way right now," TJ said, not wanting to risk a trip back down the highway to meet up with this guy.

"You trying to play me, nigga? You think you the only smart muthafucka in this conversation? I got data on you, pics I can put on the Gram and blow ya shit up, if you fuck with my money!"

Hearing Big Black speak like that sent a surge of anger rushing through TJ's body like a burning fire. His team could see the shift in his body language, his facial expressions, before he responded. "Like I said, be mindful of how you talk over these airwaves," he said, taking a deep breath. "Where do you want to meet up at?"

"Harrisburg, Pennsylvania, nigga. Like I said, I got data."

Big Black's response sent another burning flame through TJ's body. At the same time, he could feel himself along with his team being compromised, because no one they ever did business with was aware of where they were from. This fat muthafucka did his research and had a backup plan as if he was going to get burned out

4

of his share of the money.

Now TJ was regretting bringing him in on this deal. "Text me your location, so you can get this bread, and can we go our separate ways and never do business ever."

"I'm on it now. I'll see you within the hour," Big Black responded, hanging up the phone.

TJ slammed his phone down, angered by the call and his decision to bring this piece of shit in with them.

"Que paso, TJ? You don't look so good, hermano," Juan said, looking on at his friend.

"I have to take care of something. We'll link back up later," he responded before taking money out of the bag and then picking his phone up as he rushed out of the house.

Ricky looked over at Showtime and Chinaman, nodding his head. "Keep an eye on him. Make sure he doesn't need our help," Ricky said. They didn't hesitate to get their brother's back as he would for them if they needed.

TJ got into his dark blue Dodge Ram sport truck with tinted windows. Chinaman and Showtime got into the Burgundy Chrysler 300C, making a U-turn to follow TJ.

"I don't like this one bit. You know, us keeping tabs on him like we're spying and shit," Showtime said.

"This could be for his own good. Whoever it was on the other end of the phone could be the inside man, demanding more or even trying to blackmail him or something," Chinaman said, making a right turn, seeing TJ driving faster as if he knew he was being followed.

Chinaman slowed down, being alert, giving him his space, but keeping close tabs. They drove for close to twenty minutes before they saw TJ pull over at Chan's Chinese takeout in the uptown area of the city. TJ parked in front, leaving the truck running while he scanned the area.

"You think who he came to see is in there?" Showtime asked as they looked from afar, being close to a hundred yards away at the Exxon gas station on the other side of the street.

"Public place, no drama with all of the people inside, plus the traffic right here coming past," Chinaman responded.

As those words flowed from his mouth, he could see someone approaching TJ's truck.

"That's a big muthafucka right there," Show-time said. "We might have to cripple team him if shit goes wrong."

"They make big bullets for people like him," Chinaman stated, removing his gun from the side of the seat.

Big Black opened the door to TJ's truck, pausing before he got in, at the same time looking like he was reaching for a weapon.

"Is he about to pull out on TJ?" Showtime asked as his eyes widened in fear, knowing he couldn't let this happen like this. Then calming his suspicions of foul play, Big Black nodded his head, smiling at the sight of money being displayed by TJ to assure him everything was okay.

Inside of the truck, TJ and Big Black started talking. "The streets is saying y'all got away with close to a million, which means that fifty racks I was asking for went to two hundred bands," he said with greed in his eyes.

"Here's fifty as promised. As for what the streets is talking about, you can't believe everything you hear."

Big Black secured the fifty racks inside his light jacket, at the same time looking for more. "What about them bricks? The streets ain't lying about that shit. Niggas is getting tortured about that work. Plus Ballin' Bobby put a half a ticket out on the ones that came in his spot with his daughter at gunpoint," Big Black said, still thinking about more money. "Knowing what I know, you cut me in on like ten of them bricks, and we never see each other again, feel me?"

TJ started looking around, wanting to put a bullet in his face right now for the shit he was talking. "I think you should take what you came for and not allow your greed to get the best of you," he said, being calm and trying to stay in control of this situation that had already gone too far. "Don't look at me like that. Just take the money and get the fuck out of my truck!"

Big Black reacted, reaching for his gun, but not fast enough. TJ beat him to the draw, taking aim at him with his 9 mm with the laser beam pointing center mass.

"Don't lose your life over something that isn't yours. You got paid, now forget that you ever met me," TJ told him.

Big Black reached for the door handle, opening the door and stepping out with his eyes locked on TJ. "You really fucked up, nigga! I'm going to blow your spot up with this shit on the Gram, and that nigga Ballin' Bobby is going to come at all you muthafuckas!"

TJ was thinking fast, trying to process this situation that was now out of control. If he was anywhere else he would have killed him already, but the traffic was high. Back across the street, Chinaman and Showtime could see the aggression on Big Black's face as well as his body movement, which meant something was wrong.

"This doesn't look too good. He's holding his jacket, clenching the money," Chinaman said.

"I bet that piece of shit wants more money. This is why it wasn't good for him to bring someone from the outside in on this job. Plus, how did he find us and our city?" Showtime said, feeling angered and exposed, knowing they had to protect this double life they lived by any means necessary. Chinaman glanced over at Showtime, processing his last words, now realizing how deep this shit was. TJ must have slipped up, and he followed him back to the city. Either way, they couldn't let him leave this way.

As these thoughts were rushing through Chinaman's head, Big Black slammed the door and rushed off walking toward the back side of the plaza. Chinaman took off driving toward the direction he saw Big Black disappear. "We can't let him leave the city. He found TJ somehow, which means he knows enough to expose what we have going on, feel me?" Chinaman said. At the same time they could see TJ driving off angry at himself for allowing this even to take place.

Chinaman, driving slowly, followed Big Black to his Dodge Charger with the white racing stripe. Big Black started looking around before getting into his car, which he parked by the dumpster so he wouldn't be seen on his approach in case TJ had other plans. Once he got into the car, Chinaman mashed the gas, racing up behind his Charger and blocking him in. He jumped out, making his way over to the driver's side, still undetected since Big Black was looking down into the bag of money like it was Christmas. Chinaman tapped on the window, startling him at the same time getting his immediate attention. His eyes widened, seeing this Asian man staring back at him with a sadistic smirk. His hood instincts made him reach for his gun. At the same time Chinaman pressed his .44 Magnum snub nose up against the window, squeezing the trigger and unleashing a thunderous round. It pierced the glass and slammed into his skull with enough force to push half his body into the passenger side with chunks of his brains and skull, sucking the life from his flesh. He'd have no more thoughts of getting money or setting anyone else up to be robbed. Chinaman reached over and took the bag of money before calmly walking back to the car as if nothing ever happened. From what he could see, no one was around or even looking. He got in the car, racing off.

"TJ will be happy to see his money again," Chinaman said.

"We should split it since he compromised us."

"Yeah, but we're going to give it to him so he knows we always got his back no matter what. Besides, he would have killed him for us."

THREE

Back at the stash house, TJ was explaining to the others his sudden exit from the spot earlier. As soon as Chinaman and Showtime came through the door, TJ noticed the bag of money he had just given Big Black. Chinaman tossed him the money as he said, "We don't take losses, nor do we invite people into our circle. Less is more, Like Jay-Z says." TJ couldn't help but take notice of the specks of blood on the outside of the bag. He placed the bag on the floor alongside his feet.

"I see you created another problem, from the looks of it," TJ said, referring to the blood spatter.

"No, he was the problem, and I made it go away. You should be thanking me for the money and making him go away. Besides he's from out of town. No one will miss him. His homicide will run its course. You know this city and how it works. No one ever sees anything. I left him by the trash where he belongs."

"Now that we have that out of the way, we do have another thing to take care of," Ricky said.

"We don't usually do two back-to-backs in the same weekend," Juan said, knowing they just did a job. Being away from their families too much would cause questions to arise.

"There's a reason we all take time in between jobs. It allows us to do research on the targets and the locations," Jay stated.

"We own the night because they never see us coming," Ricky responded. "We take advantage of the unexpected, and then, poof, we're gone, just like that, and them muthafuckas will never know what hit them," he added, trying to see if they were on board with him in this next job.

This required the entire team to make it work. "Whatever happened to 'we ride together anytime together,' like Chinaman and Showtime held TJ down today?"

Each of them had their arms crossed processing all that had taken place over the last twenty-four hours. They also knew that greed could get the best of any man. None of them wanted to fall weak to greed. However, they all got a rush out of being takers of the night, jacking kingpins and goons for their riches and product.

Breaking the silence in the room, Jay spoke up, "I'm in with brother. Then after this, I'm done. We have made more than enough money, plus we still have the product to make more money." Each of them looked at him, shocked by his statement but respecting his decision to get out of the lifestyle they were living in secret. Jay was more family-oriented, having a wife and five-year-old twins. He wanted to start enjoying his money and family, taking vacations. So for him it all made sense to get out while he was ahead.

"I'm in," Chinaman said. "Y'all know I love this shit." He smirked before drinking his beer.

"Me too," Showtime added.

"You already know I'm all in," Juan stated.

"I guess we need to get suited up for this shit. Where we meeting up at?" TJ asked.

"Spanish Harlem," Ricky responded.

"Really, New York? That's three hours away plus recon," Juan said, knowing that time wasn't on their side.

"We move in the night. We have until 5:00 AM to be in and out," Ricky said before taking a few gulps of his spring water. "Besides, from my intel it should be a smooth job. There's a few guys keeping watch at night. We can handle them."

Each of them had their man on the inside giving the intel on these kingpins along with other corrupt street figures. As they geared up mentally for this next job, each of their cell phones sounded off, getting their immediate attention. "This isn't good," they were thinking.

"So much for having a day off. The chief just called us all in for a cop shooting," Ricky said, shaking his head. He really wanted to take out this next score in New York, but duty called, which meant they had to worry about that at a later date. Each of them were local police officers with the Harrisburg Police Department, except for Ricky and Jay, who were detectives. They all met up years ago when they were in the US Marines on the front line. Now back in the States, they were still chasing that rush of being at war. "For those that have been drinking, make sure you brush your teeth or freshen up, so the chief doesn't send you home," Showtime said.

"I'll see y'all at the station," TJ said, exiting the house, making a call to his wife so she knew he had to go in for work. The others did the same, knowing a cop shooting could turn into an all-day job.

"Everything happens for a reason. We're definitely going to take down that stash house this weekend coming up, or on a weekday, as long as

we're back before our shifts start," Ricky stated,
seeming anxious, as if the score they just did
wasn't enough for him. Each of them made it to
their cars angered at the thought that one of their
own had been killed. The chief hadn't said who the
officer was that lost their life. More than likely they
would know who it was since they had a close-knit
police station. With this taking place, they now had
to shift their mindsets to officers in blue, instead of
thieves of the night robbing and jacking drug
kingpins.

FOUR

Within the hour the team found themselves inside the large conference room with uniformed officers, homicide detectives, and undercover drug detectives. The chief of police was there, as well as the shift commander, Ivan Holland, who was a forty-nine-year-old, light-skinned Afro-American standing six four, with thick eyebrows, a full beard, and an Afro. Soon as they entered the room, they could feel the tense vibe as they stood in the back of the already crowded room.

"Now that everyone I called seems to be here, I'll begin," Captain Holland said, taking hold of a clipboard, looking down at the information he had along with the picture of the downed officer. "This city has seen its fair share of homicides alone, but when it's a fellow officer, we have to clamp down on this city and the goons that run our streets to get resolve," he said before taking the remote and tapping the On button to the large 65-inch flat-screen mounted to the wall behind him. "This isn't just a fellow officer of arms," he said, now displaying the officer's picture. "This officer is an undercover drug task force detective out of Baltimore."

As the words from his mouth stopped, the image became clear to Chinaman, TJ, and Showtime, who'd all seen this guy up close and personal. Chinaman's heart seemed to jump, doing flips inside of his chest, knowing he was the one that killed this detective. Yet on the outside he remained calm, knowing he couldn't go down for this or be on death row for this. TJ and Showtime simultaneously sucked in a heated deep breath, looking at one another. "This is Detective Marlon 'Big Black' Kemp. Once we ran his plates and ID, we found out he was working an active case that led him to Pennsylvania. Now his superiors are looking into what he was chasing down in our city. This is where we as fine officers come in. I want all ears to the streets. I want officers, detectives, and any CIs you guys have to look into every corner of the hood until we come up with answers."

Captain Holland continued his in his deep voice, "Detective Kemp was a remarkable officer, with three kids and a wife that he left behind in the line of duty. So we as his fellow officers owe him, his wife, and his children justice by finding his killer."

"Captain, sir, so if and when we do track down this murderer, since he took one of ours, he's considered armed and dangerous. So dead or alive would be justice for his family?" Chinaman said. Some of the officers agreed with what he was saying in a low tone. Even the captain understood the grief and anger of the men, yet he had to remain professional.

"Alive, so he or she can stand trial."

Showtime and TJ looked on at Chinaman as he stood there with a sadistic smirk on his face. Seeing this gave them an eerie feeling about their long-time friend. They thought that even with him knowing he killed a fellow officer, he was getting a kick out of it, enjoying the rush of murder. TJ was now shaking his head, processing the conversation he had with Big Black about the city knowing how much money and product they took. The other thoughts entering into his mind were why the Baltimore task force didn't just bust Ballin' Bobby's stash house, to get the seize and bust on paper. Then it hit him: Big Black was a crooked cop that wanted a piece of the street life. His greed cost him his life. Call it karma.

"Chief Jacobs, would you like to add anything, sir?" Captain Holland asked, stepping aside. Chief Jacobs was a sixty-year-old wise fella who had been around for years and knew the streets of Harrisburg and other cities around the state.

"Ladies and gentlemen, it's never good when we have meetings like this. Now I ask that you look at the officer to your left and your right. Now look up at this screen and visualize their faces on it. He may not be from this city, but he's one of ours. He's family, and we have the obligation to find his killer," the chief said in his heavy, drawn tone as he was staring out at the crowded room of officers.

The large six-foot-even, two hundred forty-pound old guy was a force to be reckoned with. "I want to check all cameras in the immediate area of this shooting. I want officers knocking doors. If they have one of those Blink or Ring doorbell things, I want it checked."

Hearing this sent a spiking fear through TJ and the crew, knowing none of them checked the area for the Ring doorbells. Ricky, Jay, and Juan, looked on at the others and saw that something was wrong amongst them, but right now they were going to wait until this was over with.

"Time is of the essence in solving a homicide

within the first twenty-four hours. With that being said, you are all dismissed to begin your shifts, including overtime for those of you that weren't scheduled to work today," the chief said before stepping away from the podium. The remaining officers and detectives exited while discussing the homicide and why he was in their city unannounced.

Ricky and his team made their way through the other officers to a more secluded area before he started questioning them. "What's going on, TJ? I see you and Chinaman looking as if you know something."

Chinaman looked at TJ before Showtime blurted out, "That was the inside man."

Hearing this sent fear through the others, knowing Chinaman and how he resolved it for him trying to expose them.

"No one knows what we know, and we keep it that way. We stay ahead by staying informed and alert at all times when it comes to this case," TJ responded.

Ricky, being the mastermind of the crew, knew he had to stay on top of this, because getting exposed or having any of his team fall was not an option.

"TJ, muy loco Chinaman," Juan said, shaking his head. "We should go to the hood to see what they know. It's best we be kin the front line instead of being in the back waiting on info to trickle down to us."

"He's right. We'll all hit that area and check fifty yards out for doorbell cameras as well as witnesses," Jay said before making his way out, knowing homicide already left the police station an hour ago.

FIVE

TJ, along with Jay, was sitting in his car looking on at the homicide detectives talking to potential witnesses. He was trying to figure out which of them spoke with the homicide detectives the longest. These would be the people that had something to say or thought they saw something.

"Look at big momma right there. You can tell when she heard the gunshot she was on the floor scared," Jay said, profiling her as she was talking with homicide gesturing her hands and shrugging her shoulders, followed by the look on the detective's face as if he came to a dead end. The detective's eyes veered off to the left, seeing another female standing to the side with her hands on her hips wanting to talk to him. The detective hurried up with big momma, not wanting to lose this female looking as if she was about to walk. He waved her over as he flipped his notepad out, becoming attentive as she spoke.

Chinaman and Showtime saw this as well as TJ and Jay. "Watch this genius move right here," Chinaman said, driving over to where the detective was but in a different car from before. He came to a halt and jumped out with Showtime.

"What is this folk doing?" TJ asked as he was looking on at Chinaman.

"He better be helping instead of hurting this

situation even more," Jay said.

Chinaman along with Showtime approached, flashing their badges since they were still in street clothes. "I'm Officer John Lee, and this is my partner Sean Jones. The chief asked that we help on this case in any way possible. I see we have a potential witness here?" Chinaman questioned, somewhat sarcastic. The female did a double-take as she looked on at Chinaman. She knew what she originally saw, but now she was questioning her judgment and perception.

"Ms. Price was informing me that she saw a man jumping out of a car walking up to the victim's car," the detective said.

"His name is detective Marlon Kemp, but I know you're used to saying victim," Showtime stated.

"Now that you two have that out of the way,

what does this guy you saw look like?" Chinaman asked, staring at her intently. Her mind and heart were racing trying to grasp what was going on. If this guy in front of her was the killer, then he was a good guy doing bad things. This city already didn't trust the police, now this. If he was not the killer and she said it looked like him, then it could fall back on her.

"He looked like you, I mean an Asian man, I think," she responded, confused and now scared.

"You can't think. You have to be sure, because there is an officer dead. If you say an Asian man, there is Chan's right there. Now you sure you saw what you saw?" Chinaman asked, placing pressure on her.

"I heard a loud gunshot, which made me look in that direction. That's when I saw a man that looked Asian get into his car with a bag or something in his hand," she responded.

The detective took over the questioning. "So if you saw this guy again in a line-up do you think you could ID him?" Chinaman looked on at her checking her body language, at the same time mad at himself for slipping on a move like this, not being duly aware of his surroundings.

"I, I don't know. I wasn't close up or anything like that. I just saw the person walking away from the car. I'm sorry, I thought I was helping you with this," she said, now doubting herself and what she saw, especially with Chinaman staring her down, making her feel uncomfortable.

"I know how things like this can be, especially with the pressure of the moment. Here's my card if you remember anything else that stands out to you," the detective said, extending his card for her to take.

At the same time Chinaman snatched the card before adding, "I'll write my number on the back in case the good detective doesn't pick up or isn't available at the time." He handed the female the card. "Don't hesitate to call. We need to close this case."

Chinaman said this with a smile that didn't match the darkness in his eyes. This alone sent fear through her. Right then she knew she wouldn't be calling him or anyone involved in this case. She didn't want to risk her own life trying to be a good Samaritan. Showtime could see the look of anxiousness in her eyes, wanting to get as far away as possible from them.

"Okay, it's time for me to get back to my baby," she said, hurrying off.

"Yeah, we wouldn't want anything to happen to your baby with all that is going on out here,"

Chinaman added before turning to the detective. "If you need anything, me and my partner are more than willing to help. We want to solve this thing." As those words flowed from his mouth, TJ and Jay pulled up accompanied by Ricky and Juan in their cars.

"No cameras in those houses over there. As for the plaza, all of the cameras are pointed down at the back doors, none that can see where the car was parked," Ricky said.

"Somebody had to see something out here," the detective said, looking around, knowing drug dealers were out here trapping. "Nobody is going to be getting money out here until we get answers," he added.

"We got your back if you need anything," TJ said before nodding his head to Chinaman, signaling him to get back into his car to leave.

"Anything we can do, it'll get done from our end. We can see what the CIs know."

"Any info can help close this case. I'll see you men later. I have to make my rounds to see what I come across."

Once he was out of earshot, Ricky pulled alongside Chinaman's car. "Aye, tone it down a bit, because if I didn't know better, I would think you like this situation we're in. I say *we're* because we are a team. No missing links in our chain of unity. We need you there at all times, so stay focused."

"Loud and clear, sir," he responded, knowing as Marines he outranked him.

"Let's look around a little more to see if we missed anything. Then we go spend time with our families," Ricky said, staying focused as always.

SIX

Four days after Detective Kemp was murdered in cold blood, a witness came forth IDing China-man with a cell phone video made by two teens filming a rap video for their social media page. They took notice of the background action, vividly seeing the Asian man walking up on the car, pulling the trigger before reaching into the car and taking out the bag of money, then walking back to his car calmly as if nothing ever happened.

A small handful of people saw this video and wanted to keep a lid on it, waiting for Chinaman to come to work since he was scheduled for today. Little did the detectives know Ricky had an inside man that informed Jim of this newfound footage. Chinaman was already on his way to work, unaware that homicide detectives were now at his home in case he doubled back. Juan, Jay, Showtime, and TJ weren't aware just yet. Ricky wanted to make sure he didn't spook the team. He called Chinaman, who was now a few blocks from the police station. The phone rang a few times before going to voice mail.

"Pick up the phone if you don't want to go to jail," Ricky said, not wanting his associate to get caught. He redialed the number as thoughts started filling his head—all of the shit going wrong if they got ahold of him. His team would have the spotlight on them. This time around he picked up the phone.

"What's up, Ricky boy?"

"A jail cell and death row if you're going to work."

Hearing this, he hit the brake. "What the hell does that mean?" he questioned, thinking about losing his freedom and this good life.

"They know it's you, John," Ricky responded.

Chinaman knew this was real from the tone and seriousness in his voice. He pulled over as his heart rate surged, forcing his mind into overdrive. "I'm not going to jail, Ricky. How do they know it's me?"

"Two kids shooting a video for social media caught everything. It's HD clear, John. Remember, be calm and don't panic. We have all of this under control. Go to the secondary hideout, and we'll all meet you there. Get you a go bag, fake IDs, the works to make sure you can leave the country and never look back. There's no time to slip up. Just go and we'll meet you there," he said, hanging up the phone and making his way to the highway that led to the hideout in Lancaster County close to forty miles outside of Harrisburg— far enough to get him prepared to leave the state and country.

As Marines they didn't panic or allow anything or anyone to compromise them in any way. Ricky was closer to the hideout than Chinaman, which gave him time to get things in order, make the call to the others, and make sure no one else was there. With the hideout being in Amish country with a few hundred acres, they wouldn't be seen by anyone if an APB was put out.

Chinaman was now racing down the highway

thinking about how this shit all played out and how one muthafucka making a bad choice caused this domino effect. As he was driving he thought about calling his wife to wish her well, but he fought off the urge to do so. Suddenly his cell phone sounded off. He checked it, seeing the incoming call was from the captain at the station. Now his heart was really racing, as each second it was becoming more real to him that if he didn't leave the country, he was going to jail. He ignored the call, and then it sounded off again. This time it was his wife.

"What the fuck is going on?" he shouted out, looking down at the phone between looking ahead at the cars he was passing. "I love you, Wendy, but I can't answer this phone and you know this." He let out a deep breath, took hold of his phone, and rolled down the window. He took the battery and the SIM card out before tossing each component out as he continued to drive, having thoughts about how TJ's mistake forced his hand. He kept checking the rearview mirror to see if he was being followed. At the same time he had one hand on his gun in his lap. He knew that when they came for him it'd be with the special SWAT team, knowing he was a trained Marine.

He finally made it to the winding road that led to the hideout. When he pulled into the long driveway, he could see the multiple backup getaway cars they had there for emergencies, like now. He would be using one of these cars, plus he would be using a disguise to change his overall look. Once he parked and exited the car, he could see Ricky coming out of the house with two glasses of brown liquor. Chinaman now thought about this good life he was about to leave along with his band of military brothers.

"I'm sorry about this shit. I did what we're trained to do, to protect this thing of ours," he said, racing up the steps to the house.

"No need to apologize, brother. We do what we need to do to survive," Ricky responded, extending the other glass of bourbon to him. "This will take the edge off a little before you head out on the road."

"If I wasn't driving, I would drink the entire bottle to calm down," he responded. "To this life we live," he added before downing the double shot, feeling the warmth of the bourbon flowing down his throat into his chest.

"Come on in. I have everything you need ready to go. The team should be here any minute. They didn't want to come all at the same time. It would look suspicious since the department knows we're all tight."

"So when did the video come in? I wish I could have gotten to it before they did, to put fear in those kids."

Hearing him say this made Ricky shake his head, knowing that they were in this situation because of this fast-acting demeanor. It was good when they were in Iraq because being first meant being alive. That shit didn't work here in the civilian world. He glanced down at his watch, knowing that time was of the essence in this critical situation. "You have less than an hour to jump on the road before they realize you're not coming into work."

"I wanted to see my Marine brothers off, but if I want to see any of you ever again and not from a jail cell, I better get going," he responded, picking up the go bag Ricky had prepared for him.

"The disguise is inside the bag along with the

fake IDs and credentials. There is a half a million in the bag, mainly fifties and hundreds. There's a card in there you can use with five grand on it in case you don't want to pull out the cash. Also, if shit hits the fan, there's the cyanide pill to end things on your own terms."

As those words flowed from Ricky's mouth, Chinaman felt a jolting pain surging through his body. At the same time his eyes widened as if he was being constricted by a large python. He gasped for air as his teeth clenched down hard trying to embrace the pain. He'd been poisoned by his Marine brother.

"Oh, I must have put the pill in your drink thinking ahead as we Marines do to not be compromised as you've done, and we can't let this go on with you out there running wild being who you are."

White foam started permeating from his mouth as he was being pulled closer to the darkness of death. Chinaman, in his last attempt, tried to reach for his gun to get a shot off, all to no avail. His body started shaking and convulsing violently as the remaining life slipped away from his flesh.

"I'll see you on the other side, brother," Ricky said, pouring himself another glass of bourbon and chugging it. "Aggh, this is the good stuff, my friend," he said, coming back over to Chinaman's body and removing his ID tag before placing it around his neck and tucking it into his shirt. Then he picked his lifeless body up and carried him around to the large barn where he had a fifty-gallon drum of sulfuric acid H_2SO_4, a highly corrosive, dense, oily liquid capable of disintergrating a body and making it vanish from the face of the earth. Chinaman's body sizzled as he pla-

47

ced it inside the drum, allowing the acid to do its work. Then he got the car and brought it around, to hide it. Chinaman was officially off the grid and would never be found. Only he and his team knew about this spot, and they were not a threat to him or the secret life they live.

SEVEN

Twenty minutes into his ride back to the city, Ricky's cell phone sounded off, getting his attention. He could see that it was TJ, so he answered the call. "Tell me something good, my friend."

"They know about Chinaman. They're blasting that shit all over the news. That muthafucka is going to take us all down with his bullshit!" he snapped, almost losing his breath, full of anger and excitement at the fear of it all coming to an end.

"Calm down, soldier. This isn't how we react to this situation. We stay in control by staying calm. We see what others don't see. We think ahead. We plan even farther. We're Marines first, then cops and goons," Ricky stated, displaying leadership.

"We have to find him before they do and get him out of the country."

"He's already gone and far away from all of this. They'll never catch up to him now. All we have to do is deny knowing his whereabouts that day. We know nothing about that day it took place or why he did what he did. If they ever ask. Keep in mind we're officers of the law too."

"I'm going to finish out my shift. I'll see you all afterward."

"Good, we can talk about our invite to the big

city," Ricky said, still keeping his plans and focusing on the next job.

"What?"

"We don't compromise; we improvise, soldier. We move on that big-city thing Friday night. We'll be home for the cookout and the grilling of steaks and drinking a few brews."

"I'll call you later," TJ said, hanging up.

Ricky didn't like the tone of his voice as he ended the call. Although tensions were high, he was feeling the need to pull his team together to make sure everyone was focused and on the same page. Ricky pulled off the exit, merging back into the city, thinking about how much money he was going to make on the next job—enough for them to fall back for a while and live the normal life of hard-working police officers. They would have to figure out other ways to get that war adrenaline rush.

Once in the city, he made his way home to his townhouse. He noticed a black Tahoe truck with two men inside sitting out in front of his place. This didn't look good. "Could they be here for him? Was this homicide? May be the Feds? Why?" he was thinking as he drove past them to get a better look, checking the plates. He drove around to the other side of the complex and parked his car before walking back around. The truck was gone. Who were they, and what were they doing? He was being somewhat paranoid. He started looking around, making sure they didn't park somewhere else. They were gone, nowhere in sight. He rushed up the steps to his place and made his way inside, hoping his family was okay. Once inside he removed his sidearm.

"Deborah! Junior!" he called out. It was quiet

as he made his way up the steps. His heart beat fast, and he was thinking the worst. At the same time he was questioning who those men were. He made it to the top of the stairs over to his son's room. He opened the door and saw that he was sitting in front of his TV playing the PS5 console. That gave Ricky a sense of comfort as he waved to his son.

He shut the door and headed to his bedroom, putting his gun up once he heard his wife's voice gossiping on the phone. As soon as he opened the door, she seemed to be ending her call as she gave him a smile. "Here he is now coming in, in one piece, thank God. I call you later." She hung up the phone before continuing to speak with her husband. "Did you see that cop all over the news for killing another cop from out of town? How unsafe does that make the people in this city?"

"I don't know, but you're safe here with me and the kids," he said, leaning in and placing a kiss on her lips. Deborah, a biracial beauty with light skin had the best of both worlds with her hazel-brown eyes, long flowing brown hair, and dimples in her smile that exposed her pretty white teeth. She, like the other wives and girlfriends, would never know about the secret double life her husband lived. Ricky's five-year-old daughter, Angel, came running into the bedroom and jumped up on him.

"Hi, Daddy, I love you because you keep the bad guys away from us," she said with innocence in her voice and eyes. If only she knew that the bad guy was the one she was holding onto with love.

"I love you too, princess. Now, Deborah, I think we should go on a vacation after this weekend, so get online to see if you can find a place we'll all love and enjoy together."

"Is there anywhere particular you would like to go?"

"Somewhere warm. The rest you can figure out; make it a family surprise."

She could see something was bothering him. She picked up on his body language and kiss, but she didn't want to say anything at this very moment. She knew his job stressed him out at times, plus his time in the Marines made his mood and demeanor shift every now and then.

"While you figure all of this out, I'm going to take a shower," he said, leaning in for another kiss.

"I can join you if you like?"

"I would like a lot of things, but with our kids running around in the daytime like this, we wouldn't be able to have the fun you have in mind.

Tonight, if you're still up for it, I'm all yours."

"If you don't fall asleep first," she said, making him laugh as he placed his daughter on the bed and made his way to the shower to collect his thoughts. He needed to stay ahead of what was to come, since Chinaman brought heat to the city and maybe their team.

EIGHT

1:42 AM Spanish Harlem

Ricky and the team were all in black fatigues blending into the New York night, hiding in the shadows as they closed in on their target. The time was now while most of the city was out enjoying the night at clubs, comedy shows, and concerts. They moved up the fire escape with silenced weapons ranging from 9 mm to 10 mm

Colts. They came to play hard and fast to get the money that would allow them to take off for a year or longer. The intel informed them that there should be no less than a million dollars cash up in there. With this amount of money, they figured a few people would be present, nothing they couldn't handle. They had the element of surprise on their side. They also moved with military precision as they came to a window that led into the apartment.

"TJ, see if it's open first," Juan whispered, thinking it would be best to try that before breaching the window with force. He did just that, and the window was open.

"You got to be kidding me," TJ said softly, shocked that the window to a place with large sums of money was open. He opened the window and stuck his gun and head inside, parting the curtains. Nothing, no one in sight. It was the kitchen area. He entered, followed by the others.

Once the team was inside, Ricky directed them using his hands, wanting to remain silent. Intel said the money was in the main bedroom, so that's the area they'd target first. They fanned out, sweeping through the halls of the apartment.

Then it happened. A door from one of the rooms came open, the light from the room illuminating the hallway, and a female exited. She saw the men in the hall with their guns out. In the brief milliseconds it took for her to process what was going on, fear leaped through her body, followed by panic, knowing she had to alert everyone in the apartment that they were about to get robbed. "Ahi Dios mio!! Rico, these maricons is trying to rob you!" As she yelled, she tried to run back into the room to no avail.

Juan reacted fast. Squeezing his trigger, he sent silent slugs through the air, taking her down, dropping her in the doorway of the room she tried to flee back into. At the same time the others spread out fast as trained to prepare themselves for what was next.

"Mata lo!" a masculine voice boomed from the bedroom throughout the apartment. Right then two Latinos came rushing in with their guns out ready to kill someone, until they were greeted with center mass slugs dropping them in a forward tumble.

The female Juan shot was pulling herself into the room. "Papi, ajudame!" Salina pleaded for help, fearing she was going to die from her bullet wounds. Ricky and Juan closed in on the room while Jay took point at the top of the hall. The others continued on through the apartment, securing it. The female was pulled into the room before the door slammed, concealing her and whoever she was with. This only added to the equation of endless scenarios, as now they could be calling for more help. A kingpin like Ricardo "Rico" Rodriguez, born in Ponce, Puerto Rico, would never call the cops. He would rather shoot it out. With him being the most powerful kingpin in the city since Young Pablo, his pride wouldn't let him bow down to any man. He also knew they would have to breach the door to get to him, which gave him time to call up his goons.

"On three, we move," Ricky said, hearing Rico talking aggressively over the phone. They didn't come this far to go home empty-handed. Jay kicked in the door with force, followed by a concussion grenade. Then he moved out of the line of fire coming from Rico's 9 mm Uzi. As soon as the concussion grenade erupted, they all rushed in, taking aim and dropping Rico with two double taps to the face, ceasing his murderous thoughts. The female tried to grab his weapon to avenge him, until she was gunned down. No matter how pretty she looked to them, she was just as deadly.

"Search the room. The money has to be here," Ricky said as he flipped the mattress that exposed large vacuum-sealed bags of money.

"Holy shit, look at these diamonds," TJ said, looking into the red velvet bag full of loose flawless diamonds—a form of payment that makes moving currency easier.

"Drugs aren't the only thing this guy was into," Ricky said. "Take it as a plus for us, plus bag the money."

"Aye," Showtime said, coming in to the room.

"There's bags of money in the other room."

"Take all we can carry safely. We have to move fast and get out of here before his goons come," Ricky said, knowing they were up against time.

As soon as they exited the room, abrupt loud banging came across the front door followed by loud, aggressive, Spanish-speaking voices. "Oye, abre la Puerta. Bro, it's us!" the Latino on the other side of the door said, seeming like he was ready to kick the door in.

Right then everything sped up as they rushed back down the hallway leading to the kitchen. At the same time they could hear the front door being kicked in with force, followed by the sounds of multiple voices and rounds being chambered. Once in the kitchen they climbed out the way they came in.

"Go up. We can't go down. They'll see us, and we'll be easy targets," Ricky said, thinking ahead as always. They did just that, going up toward the roof.

At the same time, the Spanish goons stuck their heads and weapons out, firing off rounds recklessly at the roof area. Juan popped back in view, firing off rounds, slamming into the arm of one of the goons and forcing him back into the apartment as his gun slipped from his grasp onto the fire escape. Once on the roof, they rushed to the other side and secured a rope to the building that would allow them to propel down the side, just as they did in the Marines. Carrying these bags of money gave them a rush as they propelled down the side, having flashbacks from when they were in war. Ricky, being the last one coming down off the rope, spotted the two Latinos racing around the corner with their guns out, yelling and firing off recklessly.

"Incoming!" he yelled out, firing off rounds as he slid down the rope. The others were already on it, taking them out with trained precision and silenced slugs that sucked the life from their flesh. Once he was on the ground, they jumped into the backup vehicle they had on the side, a Dodge Durango with tinted windows that concealed them. Just at a quick glance, they took close to four million plus the loose diamonds. This was by far their biggest take.

Once in the truck, they raced toward the Lincoln Tunnel heading back to Pennsylvania. They would make it back before sunrise to seem as if they were working the homicide case, since they all left in uniform or told their spouse they had to work. Then they linked up at the stash house and changed into their fatigues, driving their first vehicle three-quarters of the way. Then they switched to a second vehicle and continued on with their mission. Once they got back to the other truck, they would dispose of it as they always did. None of the vehicles were registered to them.

Three hours later they arrived in the city and drove up to the stash house, when TJ noticed a black Suburban truck that wasn't usually there. What stood out to him were the two occupants inside, a male and female, dressed in suit jackets from what he could see.

"That truck looks strange over there, at two o'clock," TJ said, shifting everyone's attention at the same time. This raised their awareness while piquing their adrenaline, especially Ricky's, as he flashed back to the other day when he came home and saw a similar situation.

"Do they look like Feds to y'all?" Ricky asked.

"Either that or two adults cheating on their spouses," Jay stated.

"Yeah, but why are they dressed like that on a Saturday? Where are they going or coming from?" Juan questioned as they continued driving.

"If shit ever hits the fan, we go to war, not to jail, men," Ricky said, knowing prison life wouldn't be for him or his team.

"We good, soldier. I think your paranoia is just setting in," Jay said, looking at Ricky. "Maybe it's all of the money we got that has you trippin'. We rich, muthafucka," he yelled in excitement, knowing they could finally take off for a long year to enjoy their money and family.

"I wonder where our boy Chinaman is right now?" Showtime said, not knowing he was not on the run.

"He's probably in Mexico sipping on them frozen drinks right now with a bunch of sexy Latinas," TJ said.

"He better be on the next flight out of Mexico to a nonextradition country we lined up for him," Ricky said, knowing he was dead and gone, but wanting to join the conversation to make it seem as if he was still alive.

"His family will always be taken care of by us, his Marines brothers," Jay said. "Let's go home and get some sleep before we meet up later." They did just that, securing the money and diamonds before all going their separate ways, heading home to their loved ones as if nothing ever happened.

NINE

6:47 AM, Spanish Harlem

New York homicide detectives David Black and Jack Goss were combing through the visible evidence of why this crime occurred. Bags of money were lying around with a paper trail leading into the kitchen and out the window, showing the way the robbers exited. Both detectives had been on the force for many years, putting in long hours on countless cases. This was why they picked up on this case and how each victim's body was downed.

"Look at that right there, center mass just like the ones downed on the sidewalk. This isn't your local thugs coming to take money. Whoever did this had some level of skill. These guys and the girl didn't stand a chance," Jack Goss said. The five-foot-five, 240-pound, forty-five-year-old with a clean shave was trying to preserve his youth, but the bags under his eyes showed from the longer hours and days at work.

"The rope they propelled down the side of the building with shows military training," Detective Black said as he flipped through the purse on the nightstand, taking out an ID and preparing to read her name aloud until someone else spoke up.

"Salina Sanchez," the redheaded Irish officer

said with his New York accent. "She's an aspiring model that came to the city for a few showings. More importantly, she's also the sister of the notorious Mexican cartel boss Amilio Sanchez out of Juarez," he finished, looking on at her lifeless body.

"She was also celebrating her twenty-first birthday last night. How did she get mixed up with this guy?" Detective Black asked, reflecting back to his own daughter and hoping she didn't make bad decisions like this.

"What a way to end your birthday," Detective Boss stated. "This area has cameras everywhere, so we'll contact all the owners around here to see what we get."

"Military men, partner. This is a professional in-and-out job."

The detectives gathered as much information

from the scene as possible before they let the forensic crew come in to process the scene. As soon as they exited the building, they could see FBI on the scene boasting their jackets and hats, looking for answers while pointing and staring at the rope the robbers used to propel down. Then they shifted their attention across the street where houses and businesses had cameras. They also spotted the gas station a half a block down the street. The FBI planned on retrieving all of this data. In fact, as they came across it they were having members of their team looking into it. The detectives were looking on at the agents hoping they didn't come in taking their case over. Little did they know the FBI was already investigating a five-state heist ring that involved kingpins that were all under the DEA's close watch list. They started using all of their resources to investigate the

DEA agents without their knowledge to see if there was a leak inside the agency giving up kingpins to be robbed or killed to halt their day-to-day business. The FBI conducted detailed background checks dating back to high school, college, military buddies, and more. This is also why Ricky and his crew had been noticing the unmarked vehicles with plain-clothed agents inside of them. All the agents were keeping a close tabs on people who had friends and family that worked for the DEA. Ricky and his team had a friend that worked in the DEA, and he was how they got their intel, outside of the Baltimore job. It was just a coincidence that the DEA was watching Ballin' Bobby and his crew.

"Detectives, what do you have inside?" this agent asked as they made their way over to them, preparing to introduce themselves.

WARREN HOLLOWAY

"I'm Agent Davis. This is Agents Mills and Washington."

"We have two vics with center mass shots, displaying professional marksmanship," Detective Boss said. The agents all looked on at each other, seeing the same MO from the other house homicides involving kingpins. This level of corruption having military personnel or officers taking out drug kingpins sent chills down their spines as betrayal set in.

"One of the victims is Salina Sanchez, sister of cartel boss Amilio Sanchez," Detective Black said.

"Shit's really about to hit the fan then. We'll have this guy sending every sicario in Mexico trying to find his sister's killer or killers," Agent Washington said.

"That means we have to find them before the sicarios do, or we'll have a massacre to clean up,"

Agent Davis stated.

"Once we get the feed from the cameras, it'll give us a little more direction to go in, so we can get the ball rolling on this before Amilio gets wind of this," Agent Washington added.

As those words flowed from the agent's mouth, Detective Boss received an alert on his cell phone getting his attention. He glanced down at his phone and saw that someone had taken a picture of Salina's lifeless body and posted it online with a caption that read, "Fallen Beauty. #Cartel Princess." Seeing this made his heart leap into his chest, knowing the level of stupidity it took for the person that posted this had now caused an uproar amongst the Latino communities in New York and fast spreading to Mexico. "We have to hurry on this, someone just made a stupid post of her lifeless body," Detective Boss said. At the same time each of the agents became aware of this through their earpieces, hearing other agents speaking about it. They all rushed to their vehicles wanting to get on this before it got out of hand.

Little did they know down in Juarez, Mexico, Amilio Sanchez was being made aware of his sister's death by his associate. Right then he started ordering the deaths of everyone involved. "I want all of those puntas dead one by one! I want their families and anyone who looks like their friends with them dead!" he snapped before pausing to remove his twenty-four-carat gold-plated .45 Desert Eagle with a white-pearl handle. It had the inscription, "El Mundo es to do mio (The world is mine)."

"Find out which punta pulled the trigger, cut his head off, and bring it to me!" he shouted, swaying his gun across the line of known sicarios in Mexico. Each of the stone-cold killers saw the look of pain and darkness in Amilio's eyes, filled with a murderous rage. Each of the assassins nodded their heads in acknowledgment that they were to go to the United States to fulfill this tall order to kill all responsible for his sister's death. "Five million US dollars, amigos, to take care of this family business, avenging mi hermana's death. Whatever you need—guns, more people, access to places or people—let me know, and it's done. Then finish the job," he said, filled with a burning anger that was past tears.

He left the tears to his mother, who closed herself into her bedroom on the other side of the twenty thousand-square-foot mansion that sat on over a hundred acres. Sicarios all exited the compound heading to the States via multiple avenues, some legal others illegal underground.

Either way this job was going to get done by any means. The Mexican assassins would have done the job for a few thousand American dollars, but for five million American dollars, they would kill half of the country, which meant no one would be safe.

TEN

Harrisburg, Pennsylvania, 12:17 PM

Ricky and the others all met up at Jay's place on Penn Street in the uptown area of the city. They were all out in the backyard with their kids, girlfriends, and wives, enjoying each other's time, conversation, laughter, and love while indulging in all of the savory grilled foods ranging from steaks to shrimp. All of the sides were brought by the women, each showing off their kitchen skills. While the kids ran around, the couples sat lovingly embracing this moment in time as a memory that would forever be remembered and appreciated. Jay's backyard was outfitted with all of the entertainment: surround sound playing music, big-screen outdoor TV for games or fights, a gazebo. All was going smoothly, having escaped New York last night with all of the diamonds. Each of them was still unaware of who the female was or that the FBI was investigating this case and others linked to it.

Jay was over at the grill taking a beef hot sausage off the grill and eating it as-is, no bun, just the grilled flavor. Then he made his way over to the fellas. As he was walking up, Ricky's cell phone sounded off. Ricky glanced down at his phone and saw that it was his military buddy, someone he'd kept in contact with for some time. It was the same person that was giving him his inside information, and he worked for the DEA. Jay's phone chimed as an incoming message alert came through.

Ricky took the call standing up, walking away from his wife over to the gazebo. "What's new, my friend?" he asked, thinking his buddy had another job.

"You guys really fucked up this time!" Michael Anthony said. The five-foot-eleven white male had piercing blue eyes and blonde hair cut short, flowing with his baby face he kept clean and professional.

"What do you mean we fucked up? It was an in-and-out job," Ricky responded, shocked by his old buddy's tone of voice.

"That girl, you know who that girl was?" he

said, becoming angry. Ricky flashed back to the face of the girl, nothing.

"I don't know who she is or was. What I do know is she was a threat to me and my team in that moment. You know how this thing works."

"Salina Sanchez! Amilio Sanchez's only sister. If you don't know who he is, he's the most powerful and violent cartel boss ever in Mexico's history! Like I said, you guys really fucked up!" Michael sounded shaken, and TJ now realized that the FBI was at the scene in New York. Knowing this made him fearful of all the walls closing in on him. "When you hang up, burn all communications we have. Nothing, I mean nothing can ever point back to me or this agency!" he said, hanging the phone up and leaving his military buddies to fend for themselves. Michael also thought ahead of the game. He wanted to distance himself from them. In the case the cartel did come into the picture, he wouldn't be a part of it. Little did he know that contract had already been set into play. It was just a matter of time before they found all the players connected, to fulfill it.

When Ricky hung up the phone, his boys could see something was wrong and bothering him. Had he known who the girl was, he would have given her a chance to live to prevent a fallout between him and his Marine brother Michael. However, it was done, and neither he nor his team could take it back.

"What's going, brother?" TJ asked.

"That was our military brother severing ties with us because of that female on the last job; she was some cartel boss's sister."

"Amilio Sanchez's sister," Jay said, finishing his sentence, knowing this information from the text he received that displayed her body, along with a split-screen photo of her brother. "We have to protect our families even more now in case they somehow find their way here."

"We used ski masks, dressed in all black. It's impossible for them to find out that it was us," Showtime said. "Besides, the only people that know we were there are right here."

"There's also our source, who no longer wishes to communicate with us."

"Should we worry about him?" Juan asked, looking at Ricky, knowing he could gauge it from the call he just had with him.

"He sounds like he's panicking. Last I checked, we're Marines. We remain in control and stay focused at all times."

"He's one of us. He has as much to lose as we do," Ricky responded.

"We don't break down or break up. United we stand as Marines until our last breath. We continue on each day like normal, until we're forced to shift gears. In the meantime, stay alert."

Jay's wife came over, seeing the fellas' demeanor had shifted. "Play nice, boys, there's enough food and toys for everyone," Candice said, looking up at her husband and his friends with her five-foot-one small frame, brown eyes, and loving smile.

He kissed her lips before he responded. "We are playing nice. We just planning a big vacation for our families."

She smiled before walking away and leaving them to it.

"So we good, or should I get my family and go bag ready to leave town?" Showtime asked, knowing with this cartel boss angered by his sister's murder, he would do anything to get resolve.

"I don't know about y'all, but I'm going to have another one of those bacon-wrapped shrimps on the grill. Nothing else matters right now besides food, fun, and family," Ricky said, walking away. The others shrugged their shoulders and followed suit, knowing they would be ready for whatever, when and if it came their way.

ELEVEN

Alliance, Ohio, 1:57 PM

Agent Michael Anthony was at his home preparing to leave with no chance of ever looking back. He already had his go bag as he was trained to do in situations like this. He also knew that it was only a matter of time before everything fell apart and they started coming his way, especially with him being the mastermind behind it all, never having to get his hands dirty. The FBI or the cartel, once they found him out, would be coming for him and everybody he knew and loved. The plus side for Michael was he was divorced with no kids to worry about as he gathered his things to flee. It was the long hours he put in at work that made her want to leave their relationship as it fell apart emotionally, physically, and mentally. Michael broke his cell phone into pieces before placing it in the garbage disposal.

Then he did a once-over, checking things out in the house and coming across a photo on the wall of him and his military brothers. He saluted the picture as he said, "We're Marines. We don't compromise, we improvise." He took the photo down, not wanting anything in his home to lead back to him. He disposed of it before grabbing hold of his go bag and tossing it over his shoulder.

As he was walking to the front door something came over him. Call it paranoia, but it made him halt in his tracks as if someone was on the other side of the door. He reached down by his waistline for his .357 Magnum nickel-plated with hollow points in it. He came to the door looking out of the peephole. Nothing. It made him give off nervous laughter as he opened the door and rushed over to his white BMW M6 with the sports package. Once inside, he mashed the gas and headed for the interstate, until he realized he only had a quarter tank of gas. Not enough to leave the city, let alone the state. He drove to the nearest gas station already in disguise with his fake credentials, credit cards, and bank cards, all fitting the new person he was going to be in this new life far away from here.

He pulled into a Sheets gas station and up to

the pump, getting gas before he made his way inside to get something to drink and snacks to have on his long journey. He grabbed his things before making his way over to the register and flipping out a wad of fifties and hundreds. "This is fifty for the gas, and for the drinks and snacks," he said, placing a hundred-dollar bill on the counter. "Keep the change," he added, grabbing his stuff and preparing to exit, when he took notice of two black Chevy Suburbans pulling up on his car. Right then his heart jumped as adrenaline rushed through his body, stimulating his military mindset. He prepared to go all out as he started reaching for his gun.

"That wouldn't be a good idea, Agent Anth- ony," a female voice came from behind him as he prepared to exit with his gun in hand to have a shoot-out with the agents outside. Hearing the voice coming from behind him sent chills down his spine as he turned with lightning speed ready to get his shots off. Suddenly he felt his body jerk, followed by the sound of gunfire from being hit in the shoulder. His body twisted, forcing him to release his weapon as he fell up against the door he was trying to flee through. The other agents stormed in with their weapons drawn after hearing gunfire. He could see the badges hanging around their necks as they secured him in plastic flex cuffs.

"Looks like you were in a hurry to go some-where, Mr. Anthony," Agent Tonya Marks said. He didn't even see the five-foot-five agent come into the store because he was focused on getting his snacks. The brown-skinned Afro-American had been with the FBI for years. She was also on a task force of agents investigating the multi-state robberies and killings of kingpins. They tapped Michael's house phone, but he never used it, so they placed bugs throughout the house to pick up audio of his cell phone calls, since he never used the same one and didn't have one registered to him.

They found out more when he placed the last call to Ricky. His anger and loud voice were more than clear enough for them to hear. "Agent Michael Anthony, you're under arrest for obstruction of justice, robbery, and conspiracy to multiple murders in different states crossing federal and state lines."

"You crazy bitch, you shot me!" he blurted out.

"No crying, soldier. You'll live. We need you to, so you can tell us more about this case and who all is involved," Agent Marks said.

"If you give us info leading to more arrests, it will make it easy for you, and the attorney general may cut you a deal, if she's in the mood," Agent Parker said, helping him to his feet and out of the store to the awaiting ambulance. Michael became silent, not saying a word because he didn't plan on giving his brothers up. Whatever happened to him was meant to be. He would not inflict that pain or wrath on his military family. Once he was done with getting treatment at the hospital for his wound, he would be taken back to the federal headquarters. Then he would feel the heat of being in the interrogation room until he broke or gave them what they were looking for. They had enough to bring him in, but didn't know who all of the players were because of the way he handled his day-to-day business. The agents were unaware that his arrest would cause a chain of events they were not ready for.

TWELVE

6:00 PM

"Breaking news, this just in. Federal agents stormed an Ohio location arresting DEA agent Michael Anthony, who was believed to be the mastermind of a multi-state crime ring taking down drug kingpins, which they say this agency was investigating. Now, as it has been reported to our sources, the FBI is taking the lead, furthering their investigations in the surrounding states that are involved in this crime ring. They also believe the network of robbers could be military trained and could even be police officers. I know, it's hard to believe that the people that are sworn to protect us are running around like thugs," the Asian news anchor said, looking into the lenses to connect with the viewers looking on. Those looking on at the jet-black-haired Lisa Young were now feeling unsafe hearing her report as she continued to report this news nationwide and abroad.

Down in Harrisburg, Ricky and the others were sending text messages back and forth as they, too, discovered this news. Each of them knew this was not good for them or their military brother. They wanted to attempt to break him out using their resources and skills, especially with having the mentality of never leaving a man behind. Ricky sent a message out to meet up and to be vigilant, so they wouldn't get caught slipping.

Meanwhile, down in Juarez, Mexico, Amilio was being made aware of the federal agent who had been arrested in connection with the string of robberies.

"Jefe, that punta es Federale," the Mexican thug said, speaking to Amilio and showing him a picture.

Amilio held on to the phone, staring intently at the picture of Michael. "So this piece of shit is responsible for mi hermana's death? I want him and anyone else involved to feel my pain and wrath a thousand times over!"

"Si, jefe, I'll take care of it," Carlito said, being his number two guy and a good friend to the family. He was going to make sure all of the assassins in America knew about this agent and anything they needed connecting them to the agent.

Amilio handed the phone back to Carlito when his mom entered the room, making her way over to him. "Mi hijo, tell me you found out something about your sister."

"Mama, esta bien. I have everything under control. They will pay in blood. I never let you down, Mama," he said, embracing her. This was a side of him many would never see. The only thing they would get is dark stares and death. He only trusted people in his circle he kept close, knowing he had the power that many men and women would kill for. He released his embrace from his mother, allowing her to exit the room, leaving him to his thoughts. All he wanted to do was get revenge for what happened to his baby sister.

Nothing else mattered at this point. He would give it all up to have her back right now.

Meanwhile, back in Alliance, Ohio, everyone was all in an uproar because someone leaked this information on the arrest of the DEA agent, Michael Anthony. This wasn't how they wanted to pursue closing this case. This would inform all of those involved in this case, meaning they no longer had the element of surprise they had with Michael. They also knew that due to this breach, they couldn't trust this location, because it had been compromised. They needed to prepare to move on such short notice. The plan was to move him to a more secure facility. New York had maximum facilities that would give them some comfort. Agents Marks and Parker along with the others were gathering their gear, ready to roll out—weapons, earpieces for communications.

They didn't normally move recent arrestees, but they needed to in this case before they had an onslaught of criminals trying to get at Michael for his role in this.

"After we get to New York, we need to flush out the mole that gave up this information compromising everyone," Agent Parker said, securing the weapon.

"It's time to go, Mr. Anthony," Agent Marks said as they came into the interrogation room, securing him to be escorted.

As they made their way out of the room, the agent radioed in to the awaiting transport in the garage area. "Transport, one in traffic coming your way."

"Copy that. We're all secured here," the agent came back over the earpiece. Now the level of adrenaline was high as they were making their way down in the elevator. Each of them was having thoughts, processing many different outcomes in the event shit went wrong, especially with having a leak in the agency. They were coming from the 13th floor, which made their blood pressure rise at the same time their minds were racing to process the feelings that were coming over them, since this entire thing with this agent wasn't right. The elevator started shaking as the lights were flickering. This never had happened before. Then it happened: the lights went out and the elevator halted abruptly, sending a jolting fear that something very terrible was about to take place. They braced themselves as Michael remained calm, no fear. The time for fear had passed. What was meant to be would be.

"Transport, we have a problem: the elevator just went out," Agent Parker said. "Is everyone okay?"

"I'm okay," Agent Marks responded.

"Fear is for the weak," Michael said, taunting them.

"Shut up, we didn't ask for you to speak. You'll have your chance when you're in court standing trial," Agent Marks said.

Michael started laughing. "In case you haven't been paying attention, this isn't the type of car that will ever make it to court."

"Transport, can you hear me?" Agent Parker said, hoping they could hear them, but nothing. A minute passed by, which seemed longer before the lights came in along with the movement of the elevator.

"Transport, there was a slight delay. We're coming now," Agent Parker said as the elevator came to the ground floor, chiming as the doors parted.

Each of them was on high alert as the first agent exited with his gun out, clearing the area. They moved in on the trucks that awaited. Once at the truck, they stood guard while he was secured into his seat belt. Once he was secured, they jumped into the other trucks, and the convoy took off, leaving the garage.

As the convoy drove, Michael was looking on at the federal agents driving him. They weren't the two that brought him down. They were different agents. Maybe it was to keep him and those on the outside guessing. Either way, it didn't feel right to him. He looked to the agents on his left and right to see if they, too, noticed something that was out of place with these two in the front. Nothing. Maybe they were all just new to the way shit was supposed to get done in situations like this. Their level of acuity should be high. The slightest things should stand out to them.

"Is it me, or does this feel wrong?" Michael asked the agents on his left and right. They didn't even have a chance to respond. The driver made a sharp left turn, breaking away from the convoy as the passenger turned, pointing his weapon to the back seat and firing off two swift rounds, one in each of the agents' faces. Then he pointed the gun at Michael before speaking.

"There's a five-million-dollar bounty out on you and anyone connected to you. Being Feds, we find out all the good stuff pretty much as soon as it happens, and we're looking to collect on you dead or alive," the now-crooked agent said. "I know you're not fazed by the blood splatter, but it had to be done. Now we turn you over for the money."

The agents didn't realize the cartel or their

sicarios weren't going to negotiate with them. They did the dirty work, and the assassins would keep the money. Hearing this added more concern, because he didn't want to go to jail, but definitely didn't want to be turned over to the cartel to be tortured. As he was having these thoughts, the other agents did a U-turn, seeing that the truck had broken off from the convoy. The crooked agents turned into a dark alleyway before coming to a halt.

Michael could see the Mexicans all standing by their cars with guns out. "Not good, this can't be happening," he thought. "You two don't know what you're getting into," Michael said, seeing the goons approaching and wishing he could change their minds because it was not going to go well for them or him. They should know better.

"What's done is done, my friend. We're in it for

the money. Just like you and your team," the rogue agent said as the Mexican goons and hitmen approached the truck, guns in plain sight in case shit didn't go their way. Each of them was boasting the gang tattoo MS-13. Seeing this, Michael feared the worst, knowing their violent reputation. The one seeming to be in control approached the driver's side looking serious with murder in his eyes.

"You got that punta, or what?" he asked, leaning to get a glimpse of Michael in the back seat.

"You got our money?" the rogue agent asked as the Mexican continued staring down Michael. Michael could see the pure evil in this guy's eyes. He knew that these rogue agents were way out of their league fucking with these murderous Mexicans.

"Oye, give these gringos their money," he ordered. Then the one with the bag in his hand came up approaching the truck. Suddenly he dropped the bag, exposing the MAC-11 machine gun and spraying into the faces and bodies of both agents, slumping them over as the life left their greedy, corrupt flesh. Once he let up off the trigger, the others closed in, opening the back door to secure Michael.

"You can die of torture or a quick death depending on what you tell us about the others that helped you. Your parents have a lot to lose, too, if you don't tell us what we need to know, amigo. We have people at the retirement community right now ready to cut them up piece by piece, punta." He couldn't bear the fact that harm could be brought to his parents.

"Whatever you need, just don't hurt them," he pleaded, not realizing his parents were dead, already in the trunk of the car he was being placed in.

THIRTEEN

6:46 AM, Harrisburg, Pennsylvania

Jay was at his home wide awake after seeing the news about rogue agents attempting to break Michael out only to become victims themselves. This only showed him and the rest of the world looking on how violent these cartel hitman could be. The news even showed the graphic aftermath of the crime scene, giving those on the outside a vivid look into how the cartel operated. These MS-13 contracted assassins along with other Mexican sicarios didn't value life, only money, power, and loyalty for whoever contracted them. It just so happened to be a notorious, billionaire, murdering cartel boss from their home country.

Jay sat in his living room with his go bag contemplating leaving now, but having twin daughters and a wife, it was hard. Either way he had to leave, but was taking them going to place them at even more risk? Or was leaving them behind to fend for themselves any different? These were the thoughts and emotions he'd been dealing with, unable to sleep, yet knowing that time was ticking. As he sat in the dark silence, he figured they would torture Michael for information. Even if he wanted to be tough, they would find a way to get it out of him.

As these thoughts were coming to him, he whipped out his cell phone to start making a video diary documenting everything that had led to this point, even if it didn't make him look like a saint. After he was done, he took hold of his bag, tossed it over his shoulder, and made his way to the front door, before looking over his shoulder up the stairs where his wife and kids were sleeping peacefully. "I'm sorry," he said in a low whisper, feeling like a piece of shit for his life to have come to this point of walking away from all he loved. He knew if he stayed, they would die without question. He figured leaving them would give them a chance to live since the cartel would be coming for him.

As he turned the door knob, his military instincts kicked in. He let go of it and turned around swiftly, heading out the back door and never looking back with his .44 Magnum snub nose in hand, for up-close and powerful gunplay. No one was in sight as he made it to his car a few blocks away. He jumped into his Honda Accord and took off, not even looking back. He focused on heading down South, where he would later make his way out of the country until he felt it was safe to come back.

As he was fleeing for his life, on the other side of the city, Juan was in a drunken sleep after being stressed out with all that had taken place, plus what'd been on the news. He started drinking shots of tequila chased with bottles of Corona beer, while loading all of his weapons up, ranging from a 9 mm Beretta and a .22-calibur Uzi, to a hundred-round clip H&K assault rifle, along with other guns he slept with for comfort, like the 10 mm Colt with hollow points. Suddenly bringing him out of his drunken sleep, he heard glass shattering. He jumped up, sobering by the second knowing what happened to Michael and the other agents. As he sat up, he grabbed the beer bottle on the nightstand and chugged from it, before taking his guns and securing one on his waist and another in his hand with his finger resting inside of the trigger guard.

He moved with trained precision, quietly, as he closed in on the entrance to his bedroom. He could hear Spanish voices speaking. Being Latino himself, he understood what they were saying. They were plotting their approach to kill him. These were definitely cartel hitmen, he was thinking. Adrenaline was rushing through his body as he went into drunken survival mode, ready for war as he exited his room and made his way to the top of the steps.

He heard the voices getting closer as they

were coming up the steps. As soon as he came into view, he could see two of them coming up the steps, guns out, but not ready enough. He caught them off guard, squeezing the trigger in the 10 mm Colt with the hollow points. The gun roared in the closed-in space, bullets slamming into their bodies as he hit them with head and body shots to assure their deaths, thrusting their bodies back down the steps.

He didn't know there was another until he came into view at the bottom of the steps spraying with a modified Tec-9 with a fifty-round clip. Juan dove out of the way, staying silent, not wanting to give his position away. However, that didn't stop the sicarios from shouting out. "Oye, you're not going to make it out of here alive. That pretty girlfriend of yours, she's not so pretty anymore. I cut her head off, and she still looked scared!"

Hearing this pissed Juan off. At the same time it made him aware of how crazy and murderous these muthafuckas were. Juan removed his other sidearm as he took a deep breath to bring calm to himself. He stuck the guns out in front of him and appeared at the top of the step, catching the goon in the middle of his taunting speech. He squeezed both of his triggers at the same time, sending unforgiving slugs through the air. They slammed violently into the assassin's body, tossing him back into the wall as the life leaped from his flesh. Juan remained at the top of the steps to see if there were more inside of the house. Nothing.

He moved quickly back into his bedroom, grabbing his things and placing more guns into the bag. He knew he had to get out of there before they discovered that these pieces of shit didn't succeed. Once he felt he grabbed everything, he headed out of his bedroom. He was turning to leave when a razor-sharp ten-inch blade slammed into his chest, piercing his heart. His eyes widened in fear of what was to come, plus he was shocked by the unexpected. He didn't think there were any more assassins in the house. This one came in through the second-floor window as backup.

"Es muy tarde, punta!" the goon said, letting Juan know it was too late. Then he made an abrupt turn with the knife, sealing his fate further. Then as violently as he slammed it into his body, he snatched it out, taking a step back as Juan's body fell to the floor. He spit on Juan's lifeless body before leaving.

FOURTEEN

8:45 AM

Locally and nationwide, the news of officer Juan Santos's and Agent Anthony's murders was making headlines. Agent Anthony's body was found on the edge of Pennsylvania close to Ohio. His parents bodies were lying alongside his with their hearts cut out in true cartel fashion. As for Officer Santos, they made it known that he put up a fight before his demise. TJ, Ricky, and Show-time, all aware of what had taken place, were now on high alert. They knew their time was coming to an end, and they had to get ahead of it—like true Marines would.

Ricky was at home preparing to leave as he spoke to his wife, making her aware of what was going on. "Deborah, lock all of the doors and don't let anyone in if it isn't me. Here, take this gun to protect yourself and the kids when I'm gone. Call the cops if you see people that don't look like they belong around here."

"Ricky, you're scaring me," she said, taking hold of the gun. "The kids, what about them going to school?"

"There's no time for school, Deborah. We have to keep them here to protect them."

"If they're at school away from here, then it'll

just be me and you," she said, thinking like a mother wanting to protect her babies. "Because if they're home, they will be killed when the assassins come." This double life they tried to protect and keep for so long had been exposed because of that one domino that fell, meaning the killing of the cartel princess.

"Okay, have them ready in a few minutes. I'll start the car," he said, grabbing the keys off the hook by the door. He looked out the peephole. Nothing. He opened the door, looking both ways before rushing over to the car. He stuck the keys in the ignition. Something came over him, making him halt turning the key. He stopped, jumping out of the car to look underneath it to see if a bomb was attached. Nothing. This gave him some comfort, knowing nothing was there. However, his wife was looking out the window becoming even more worried seeing his behavior.

He waved her to join him in the car. She came out with the kids. Once inside of the car, she looked over at him with love, even though she was scared, "I love you, Ricky baby," she said, sounding timid and affectionate at the same time.

"We love you too, Daddy," his daughter Angel said, smiling. He could see the innocence in her smile as he glanced over his shoulder. A part of him felt guilty for this life he chose, being a rogue officer and chasing the adrenaline rush of war along with the money that came with it.

"Daddy loves you all," he responded, managing to smile as he remained alert. As he drove off, his wife placed her hand in his lap while her other hand still clenched the .380 pistol he gave her. As he drove the ten miles to their school, it was quiet as he looked around constantly to see if they were coming.

His wife broke her silence with a suggestion, "Why don't we leave town if you think they are coming?"

"It's different because of the money, power, and men this man has, giving him a global reach. So no matter how far or fast you run, he has people everywhere," he said, finally making it to the school, still looking around staying alert.

She leaned over and kissed him with love. "I'm with you no matter what," she said, tucking the .380 into her waistline as she got out of the car, the kids joining her. As she started walking away, his cell phone sounded off, startling him. He answered, not even checking the caller ID.

"Hello."

No one said anything, a calm silence followed by light breathing. "Senor Washington," a Spanish accent came across the phone.

"That's me. Who's this?" he asked, looking around.

"Senor, you and your associates took some-thing from me and my family that can't be repl-aced."

Hearing this sent a spike of adrenaline surging through his body as he scanned the area. "I didn't take anything from you."

"Pinche mentiroso," he let out, calling Ricky a fucking liar. Ricky didn't understand since he didn't raise his voice. He didn't sense a threat. He looked around, but there was nothing or no one in sight. Then the unexpected. A van coming down the road sped up unseen by Ricky because he was busy looking for people instead of this, until the van crashed violently into the back of his car. He dropped the cell phone and the gun he had on his lap as he smacked his face on the windshield. At the same time she heard the loud clash of vehicles slamming into each other, Deborah turned and saw the van that slammed into her husband's car. Fear took over her body as she saw Mexican men running her way armed with guns pointing in her direction. Fearing harm being brought to her children, she removed the .380 pistol and squeezed off as many rounds as she could, recklessly, until she was violently gunned down. Her kids were next, never standing a chance as the barrage of bullets riddled their young flesh. This was overkill as they stood over top of her firing more rounds just because she had the heart to fire on them as they approached. Ricky didn't have a chance. As soon as the van slammed into him, they came spraying him with AK bullets until he ceased to exist. After they were done, they all took off running over any onlookers to pull out their phones. This level of Mexican-cartel-style violence on American soil meant no one involved in this case would be safe.

FIFTEEN

Fredericksburg, Virginia

Jay checked in at a motel that he would stay at until he moved on to the next location that would segue out of the country. As he made his way to his room, he was looking around seeing everyone carrying on not paying him any attention. He scanned the area to see how things were as he made his way into the room—a room which was far from the comfort he was to. A gloomy color of gray and off-white was on the walls, and the curtains were stained and had seen better days. The carpet looked like it was from a wholesale place.

This was the life he had chosen and had to deal with until he left the country. He wanted to turn around. Instead he secured the door and locked it, followed by taking a chair and propping it up under the doorknob. He figured roughing it would also take him off the radar for anyone looking for him. He made his way into the bathroom, where he became even more angered seeing the shower didn't have a curtain. He would have to figure something out for that. This place was definitely outfitted for hookers and johns.

He came back out to the open area and saw

the TV screwed to the wall to prevent thieves from stealing it. He turned the TV on CNN. He hadn't been aware of Ricky and his family until now, as he saw the reporter wiping her tears from the corner of her eyes. She just couldn't hold them back after seeing this massacre unfold, caught on the school's cameras. "Again, I warn the public that the video we've shown and are about to show is graphic. Children are involved, so you may want to remove your kids from the room if you're viewing this."

The news went to the video footage narrated by a male voice giving a play-by-play account of what was taking place, and who they believed was responsible. The footage hit home for a lot of people looking on, including the president of the United States. Jay dropped to his knees seeing his best friend and family massacred, the fear in the kids' eyes seeing their mother attempt to protect them. Now he could see why the reporter was crying, because as a mother, seeing her be so helpless against that level of violence hit the heart, taking over all emotions.

She came back on the screen, holding it together, yet still shaken up from the audio of the narrator. "These Mexican assassins, as we've learned, have been contracted to kill. Sadly, these kids were innocent bystanders in this massacre."

Suddenly shifting his attention Jay heard a thump followed by voices. He grabbed his .44 Magnum from the bed and then closed in on the door. He looked out the peephole and saw the top of someone's head. He placed the gun to the door in the place he had seen the head, at the same time pulling the hammer back, ready to fire, until he heard laughter from a female and male voices.

He placed the hammer back before going to the window and looking out to see the two kissing and fondling one another as they were going into the room next door. They didn't realize that their little moment of heated seduction had almost cost them their lives.

He walked back over to the TV to see more news, when his cell phone sounded off. It was his wife calling him. He took a deep emotional breath of air, fearing the worst for her now after seeing the news. "Could this be the reason she was calling?" he was thinking, knowing if he answered the phone it could lure him back home. It was best for him to stay away from his family in case the cartel was watching. They would know he was here if he picked up. He denied the call, tossing the phone onto the bed where he took a seat, overriding the thoughts he was having of the drunken sex that had been had on this wooly blanket and bed.

"What are you doing, Jay?" he questioned himself, staring at the TV that was now showing the president speaking on the matter of the massacre. He muted the TV because his words weren't helping at this point. He started drifting into his thoughts on how he was going to prevail in this situation.

Breaking the silence and bringing him back to the moment was his cell phone sounding off again. Seeing that it was his wife, he realized she must be scared with all that was going on, plus the fact that when she got up this morning he wasn't there. Answering the phone would go against everything he'd trained for. Not answering it would mean he would never have a chance to speak to her again. The innocence of his twins calling out to him echoing in his conscious forced him to pick up the phone and take her call. "Hello, baby."

"Baby, today was your day to make pancakes for the kids," she said, wondering where he was.

"I'm sorry, I got a little busy with something."

"That's okay. I love you, and the girls love you too." Hearing her speak made him close his eyes and take a deep breath, trying to process this.

"Have you seen the news today?" he asked.

"It's heartbreaking, especially when it hits close to home." Her words sent a striking fear through his body, knowing that she had been compromised. The cartel hitmen were in his home, and there was nothing he could do about it at this point.

"I'm sorry, baby. Tell our girls I love them more than anything."

She didn't even get a chance to get her words

out. The goon took the phone from her. "You should be sorry, amigo. Pero es muy tarde para eso. You want them to live, you come to us and save the ones you love. I don't take pleasure in killing la ninas. They are so beautiful and can grow up to be something special, understand?" the assassin spoke with his strong Mexican accent. Jay could hear the heartless muthafucka breathing into the phone. There was nothing he could do to save them, and he knew this. "Oye, habla me, I need to know what you want to do, because your family is looking at me with these sad eyes."

Jay hung up knowing he couldn't save them. As soon as he hung up the phone, the other Mexican pointed at the phone, noticing something, and he fired on Jay's wife, killing her as his twins screamed in fear. Then he gunned them down, silencing their screams before leaving, focusing on the money.

SIXTEEN

Showtime was on his way over to TJ's place with his go bag and extra weapons ranging from a silenced 9 mm with extra clips to an SK with extra clips, backed by a few grenades. They figured with Jay not answering his phone and the others being killed, they were left to fend for themselves. Together with their trained skills, they could take out as many of the Mexican's as possible. They'd been in tougher situations in combat. This was just another phase of it.

Showtime was driving down the street TJ lived on when he noticed a van parked out in front of his place with Latinos exiting with weapons in hand. One of them was carrying a large machete as he was closing in on the house. Showtime stopped his car, backing up to park, before grabbing his silenced weapon with extra clips. He took his phone and sent TJ a message alert making him aware of the approaching goons. Then he exited the car, keeping his head down low, looking ahead at them as they climbed the steps. The others went around to the back of the house to secure it. The element of surprise was how they got Ricky and Juan. Now it was going to backfire on them.

Showtime slid in between the cars, moving undetected, closing in on the van with the driver still behind the wheel. Then he popped up in front of the van, catching the driver off guard as he sent silenced rounds through the front windshield taking the life out of him as he slumped over. In the same swift motion he moved toward the house firing off more rounds into the backs, legs, and heads of the assassins on the porch, dropping them where they stood. He ran up on the porch firing angry shots off into their faces and bodies as he vented. "That's for killing my brothers!" he said as he took off running around the back side. As he was running, he heard two thunderous rounds roaring through the air. He feared they got to TJ as he closed in with caution. He turned the corner and saw the downed Mexicans. This gave him a sense of relief, knowing his message got to TJ in time.

"I got ten muthafuckas! They thought they was going to catch me slipping. Good looking on the text, brother," TJ said.

"I took out the ones trying to come through the front. We have to get out of here before the police show and the cartel realizes their goons didn't succeed."

"I'll meet you around front," TJ said, rushing back into the house to get his fiancée Lisa and son. Lisa was a five-foot-seven blonde with baby-blue eyes and a bright smile accompanied by her sexy dimples. His son took her smile; everything else, he got from his dad. When they came around to the front of the house, they could hear police sirens fast approaching. TJ rushed his family over to his hunter-green Lincoln Navigator with dark tinted windows. As soon as he got inside, he noticed two uniformed police officers' cars block-ing off the street. Showtime saw this as he was backing down the street. They were followed by two Chevy Tahoes that pulled up facing down the street. The officers jumped out of their vehicles with their weapons aimed at TJ and Showtime. At the same time the men and women of the FBI exited their trucks.

TJ and Showtime, although they were in separate vehicles, were thinking alike. This wasn't how they planned their happy ending or the good life. From here, if they gave in or up, it meant life in prison or the death penalty. Being in jail would also give the cartel and MS-13 assassins a better chance at fulfilling their contract. Showtime took a deep breath before placing the Audi S4 in neutral and allowing it to drift before slamming it into gear while mashing the gas, making a sharp turn up onto the sidewalk. TJ held his position, seeing the fast-approaching S4 racing down the sidewalk. The police officers in front of TJ saw the car coming, so they jumped into their vehicles attempting to cut him off, not realizing the opening they just gave TJ. He mashed the gas, plowing into the back side of the one cop car, making it spin out as he broke free.

The sudden shift caught the officers and federal agents off guard, making them have to all rush and jump in their vehicles to try to catch up with these two that were fleeing for life and freedom. TJ turned left in his truck as Showtime continued straightforward. Then he started making left and right turns in his fast car that would allow him to create even more space between him and the cops. He drove faster, finally realizing he wasn't even being chased anymore. The cops had focused their attention on the slower vehicle of the two, which was TJ's.

"I'm not going to let you down, brother,"

Showtime said, making a sharp turn around and driving in the direction of the sirens blaring. He closed in on them just as fast as he got away from them. He was thinking about TJ and his family. Now he was right amongst them, so he rolled down his window and fired off shots at the police cars, making them swerve and crash into one another, allowing TJ to get away. As he mashed the gas to get away himself, he noticed the helicopter keeping up with him, giving his location away to the federal agents that closed in on him. They were firing off rounds from every angle, flatting his tires and punching holes into his Audi. He lost control and crashed into parked cars, almost flipping his car. The federal agents closed in fast, all with their guns out, fingers inside the trigger guards daring Showtime to make a move that would end his life without question.

"Let me see your hands! You try anything, and you're dead!" the federal agents seemed to all yell out at the same time with their adrenaline spiked from the shoot-out and chase. Showtime started laughing at thoughts of how he and the team said their ending would be somewhere warm with frozen drinks and family, not like this.

"You can't protect me. I go in, I'm dead within twenty-four hours, and you know this!" he said. They snatched him out of the car, placing the cuffs on him. They didn't plan on failing or allowing him to be killed on their watch. Everyone was on high alert.

SEVENTEEN

Juarez, Mexico

Amilio was entering his large, sumptuous living room where his mother was viewing the American news via satellite TV. She'd been watching the massacre that had taken place along with the dead officers and rogue police for the last half hour. Her motherly instinct made her aware that her powerful son had made all of this possible, avenging his sister's death. She didn't care about him having the children slaughtered like pigs. The sicarios, once contracted, would do whatever it took to get the job done and send a message at the same time. It was the Mexican cartel's way of life.

Amilio came over placing his arm around his mother, giving her comfort. "Yo he lo dije, Mama; I told you I would take care of this. No one will be safe until they are all dead," he said, taking notice of the officer now in federal custody. "This one right here, Mama, he may be hard to get, but nothing is impossible."

"I'm proud of you, mi hijo, for staying strong and letting the Americanos see they can't get away with this."

"Anything for familia, Mama," he said, placing a kiss on her cheek before leaving the room.

As he was leaving the room, Carlito was on the phone talking to someone. "Understood, gringo. No, it's never personal; it's always business. You did what you can; now it's our turn to do as we wish," he said before holding the phone away from his ear and pointing to the phone, mouthing, "American federale." "If you decide to change your mind, amigo, it would be a great financial benefit to you. If you don't, then you are in the way of this problem we're trying to fix," he said, hanging up and leaving the agent to think of his words as well as this new position he was in. The cartel had billions at their disposal to corrupt anyone. Besides, most people they approached only had two choices: to be with them or die. Most chose the corrupt life and money.

Carlito was light skinned with black-colored eyes and hair. He was slim with a thick mustache, but clean-shaven on the sides. Being the right-hand man of the world's most violent cartel boss, he had a lot of responsibility to keep the soldiers and goons below him in check along with people outside of their circle, keeping them honest in business. He, too, wasn't a stranger to murder, having killed alongside of Amilio, making his mark while gaining respect from his boss and best friend.

"Which American was that?" Amilio asked.

"Senor Blackman with the Feds. They have one of those puntas in custody. I told him to make sure he doesn't make it through the night. If he can't do it, then our men will take care of it."

"If he's doubting his ability to fulfill what has been asked of him, then he may be a problem as well. Send someone to talk to his family in case he thinks he can betray our arrangement."

"There's two more out there. They're all ex-Marines. They killed a few of our men, the other got away, and there's another our men spoke with over the phone. They're tracking him through the GPS."

"Stupid Americans, they want to track and be tracked by one another. That's not love, it's stupidity," Amilio said, not being one for relationships, just women for the moment with no emotional attachment. He didn't want to have love in his heart for anyone outside of family, because he felt it made him vulnerable and weak.

"Perdoname, senor," his maid said as she entered the room. "You have a guest waiting to see you in the study."

"Quien es, Maria?" he asked. "Who is it?"

"The American," she said, knowing that this American was someone important to him. He exited the room preparing himself for the confrontation he knew was ahead with his American associate—especially if it was Jake Rawlings of the CIA. Jake was a six-foot-two, skinny-built white male with brown hair and eyes and a clean-shaven face allowing him to look business smooth at all times. Jake had a calm demeanor that made him seem as if he was always in control, not fearing this man that everyone else in the world was terrified of.

Jake knew at any given time he could have Amilio removed from the face of the earth using the CIA's resources, or if he was ordered by the president to do so. Even then he would give him the benefit of the doubt, as he was doing right now coming to express his concerns on the wolves he unleashed on American soil.

"Que pasa, Jake? How's the Ferrari I sent you

last week?" Amilio asked, trying to get a feel for why Jake was there.

"I wish I could say I was here to talk about how nice the car is and how I convinced the police officer not to give me a ticket for speeding, but I'm not here for that. We have bigger problems."

"Tranquilo, amigo, let's have a drink before we talk business," he said, grabbing a bottle of Hennessey XO and pouring a double shot for each of them. "Here you go, amigo. Now tell me, what brings you to my country so unexpected?" he said, dinking the shot and allowing the warmth to flow down his throat.

"For starters, I want you to know that I am beyond sorry for what happened to your sister. She was good friends with my sister, making her like family. So I understand your anger. However, my friend, your men are killing federal agents and police officers, even children. This alone gives this case its own spotlight. The kids alone have social media in an uproar forcing politicians' hands, even the president's. I don't know if you've been keeping up with the news, but it's looking bad out there."

"Those pendejos deserve to die! As for their children, I want them to feel the pain I felt when they killed me hermana!"

Jake stared at Amilio, listening to him while understanding his anger. He had every right to be upset. He tilted his glass, downing the double shot before speaking. "What's done is done. You can't go after the others. If you do, the president will use his power to bring you to an end. With that being done, there won't be anything I can do for you. Now if you put your business hat on for a second and place your emotions to the side, we can continue to make money. I can assure you that if any other agencies try to come your way, they won't succeed. However, if the CTD, CIA, and NSA get involved on behalf of the president, there is nothing I can do. Your legacy will be the only thing to talk about. All of this right here will be gone," he said, pointing to the expensive paintings and statues and then him. "Even you, amigo. I want you to be smart, because you gone means no money for me or the agency."

"If she was a white American girl, amigo, what would the president and Americans say about that?"

"It didn't happen. We have to focus on what *is* happening. Which is your sicarios running around killing everything in their path," he said, taking a cigar out of the humidor on the desk, preparing it, cutting the tip off, and taking the butane lighter to it as he puffed. "This is a premium Cohiba Republic Dominica with fresh leaves, a great smoke. You know, it's things like this that I would miss if you didn't take heed to my words, good friend." He blew another cloud of smoke before adding, "I hope by the time I make it back to the States, you will have called off your killers so we can keep our focus on making money." He came over and patted Amilio on the back before exiting his mansion.

Amilio stood staring at the family portrait with his sister in it when Carlito came in. He made him aware of what was going on. "Carlito, what's done can't be undone. My men will carry out orders as contracted. The Americans want to go to war with me, then we go to war."

"I'm with you til the end. I'll boost the amount of security to protect the compound."

"Esta bien, amigo. The Americans will try to catch us off guard," he said, now readying himself for all-out war if and when it came his way.

EIGHTEEN

Fredericksburg, Virginia

Jay was inside the motel room. He feared leaving his location knowing what took place with TJ and Showtime and the attempt on their lives. At least TJ got away. Now Showtime had to be on high alert because even in there he was a target. He also sat thinking about his wife and kids, not believing that they were dead since he didn't stay on the line for it. Having that in the back of his head was taunting him too. He hoped they at least spared his twins.

He started his video diary again. "By now you should know my name and face along with my military brothers. We fucked up bad, so if you're watching this and my family is still alive, tell them I love them so much and that I'm sorry." His voice broke at the thought of his twin daughters being massacred. "If my babies are alive with their mother or someone who understands that this all went wrong, tell them I'm sorry. This wasn't supposed to happen like this. We fucked up bad." He paused, wiping his tears away, partially shaken, not in fear for himself but his family. The room phone sounded off, interrupting him. He kept the video rolling as he answered the phone.

"Hello?"

"Sir, you have a delivery at the front desk," the female receptionist said.

His heart rate picked up. He was thinking the worst: "They found me." "I didn't order anything. You have the wrong room."

"They said the officer from Pennsylvania. I didn't know you were a cop since you didn't come in uniform." She continued speaking, but her words were a blur.

He hung the phone up, taking the Beretta PX4 Storm off of the bed, safety off, and rushing over to the window, parting the curtains. There were cars that weren't there before and Spanish-speaking voices. "Is it them?" he was thinking. He could hear knocking on the room next door. Then it became silent, no one was outside.

He started speaking into the camera. "We

didn't plan for this shit to happen like this. It all went wrong," he said, rambling on until the room phone sounded it off again, followed by loud voices outside of the room, including next door. His head was on a swivel as his level of paranoia was piqued.

Then it happened, the door came open with brute force. He fired off rounds as he yelled out. His slugs found the first Mexican assassin that entered the room, but the ones that were in the room next door zoomed in on the shouting and gunfire. They took aim from the other side of the wall, unleashing a fully automatic 9 mm Uzi and AK-47s, spraying through and shredding the walls. They found their target over and over as they sent over two hundred rounds through the wall. The gunfire came to a halt next door as they could see his body slumped on the side of the bed.

The hitman in the room stood over him firing more shots into his face making sure he didn't have any chance to live.

As the four remaining contracted killers exited the motel, the police squad raced onto the property and saw these armed thugs. At the same time the thugs just reloaded their weapons then opened fire on the police squad car. The gunfire halted when they saw another police car rushing in, and they shifted their weapons in his direction. The officer slammed the gear in reverse to evade death, not wanting to end his shift right now. He reacted just in time as the slugs crashed into the hood of his car. He got out of the way and called for backup and officers down.

The Mexican killers jumped into their car, driving off past the officer they shot at, daring him to make a move. He didn't. He just looked on at them helplessly. All his years of training didn't prepare him for this type of violence. It didn't take long before the FBI and all law enforcement were on the scene. At the same time onlookers with their phones were posting the images on social media, spreading the news fast and far.

Jake Rawlings also received an alert on his phone. "This is very stupid, my friend. You chose emotions over money," Jake said, looking down at his phone and seeing the images of the recent hit. There was no helping Amilio now.

NINTEEN

Two days after Jay's death, TJ was with his fiancée and son hidden away at her parents' winter log cabin secluded on thirty acres in upstate New York. The four thousand-square-foot cabin had a modern design with all of the creature comforts, plush furniture, and natural sunlight that doubled as a picturesque scene for the night sky filled with stars. They turned their cell phones off before removing the batteries to prevent tracking.

This allowed them to be off the grid.

"Daddy, can I get something to eat?" little Tony asked.

"Mommy is going to make us something to eat, okay, little man?"

"Babe, my parents always keep food in the deep freezer, also dry and canned goods." Lisa said, kissing him before adding, "We'll be safe here."

"I always feel safe with you," he said, being funny.

"Showtime looked after us," she said, knowing what he did allowed them to get away.

"It's what we do, no man left behind," he said, pulling his dog tag out and reflecting back to the good times. "I wish we could go back to how it was when we came home from war." Going back would mean they were all alive, and things would be different.

Over an hour later, dinner was ready. Lisa had pulled out deer steaks, canned corn, and boxed mashed potatoes, all chased down with bottles of spring water.

TJ was now feeling a sense of comfort in this moment with his family. "Mmh, you did a job cooking this with love, babe."

"Mommy always cooks with love, Daddy," little Tony said in between stuffing his mouth, not worrying about a thing.

"You're right. She loves you and me so much she can't help but to make our food with love," TJ said, making the two of them laugh as they all found a sense of normalcy in this moment. "I'm going to make this all up to you once we get to our destination far away from here," he said, looking at Lisa with love—a love his son could see in their eyes as they looked at one another. Seeing this gave him comfort.

"Let's just enjoy the time we have now. Then we can figure out all the other stuff. I'm not going anywhere without you. You're stuck with me until the end," she said, taking a bite of her steak.

"I really did do a good job with this," TJ said, meaning his little family.

"Talking like that, we might be able to make another little one tonight," she laughed, looking over at her son with love. The reality was, having another child wouldn't make sense right now, but good sex might take away the tension and stress they were having with all that was going on. "Let's see how the night plays out," she said with a smile and love in her eyes.

"After dinner, we can get freshened up and let the night run its course," TJ said.

"There are clothes up there that belong to my parents, so we'll be dressed like them after we shower. At least you'll know what we'll look like when we get their age." She burst out in laughter.

The night went smooth and quiet. They took their family time to the second floor. Little Tony was tired, and he went to sleep. This gave them the adult time they wanted and deserved, making love throughout the night as if it was their last time or as if it was going to be a long time before they got a night like this again. After the long love-making session, she laid her head on his chest listening to his heart and breathing until she fell asleep. He sat up a little longer before he, too, fell deep asleep, dreaming of better times and a better life far from this moment, minus the comfort he had with his fiancée.

TWENTY

Two weeks passed by without anyone being tracked down or killed by the cartel's hitmen. They made many attempts to get Showtime with different cellmates, all to no avail. He saw them all coming a mile away. After the many failed attempts, they placed him in protective custody.

When word made it back to Mexico that these contracted killers were failing, Amilio was pissed, wondering why the government was protecting this murderer. He was also angered they couldn't find TJ, so he set an example by taking a machete and striking with force, decapitating one of his assassins' heads just to get his point across that failure was not an option. "This is how you kill! There is no excuse for failure!" The dark, murderous stare along with the bloody head dripping got their attention.

Amilio was also angered by Jake not returning any of his calls. So much for being like family. All that had been taking place was also making Amilio paranoid. He didn't even trust the people he'd been around since day one. He'd been cleaning house to make a power statement as well as to appease his paranoia. Carlito, his mother, and immediate security detail were all he had around.

~ ~ ~

7:45 PM

The spring sky was showing signs of setting as the picturesque sunset was fading from powder-blue to night. At the same time Alpha-7, a supremely trained team of men and women with military backgrounds, along with the added training of the CIA and backed with the intel of the NSA, had been assembled on the orders of the president.

The team crossed the border one by one so they wouldn't be flagged by corrupt officials on Amilio's payroll. The compartments that concealed their weapons passed through with ease, having the highest-grade stealth technology. Each carried a .50-caliber sniper rifle, handguns, explosive ordinances, and enough ammo to stand their ground. All of their weapons were outfitted with silencers to enhance their stealthy maneu-vers when closing in on the target. As for nonlethal weapons, they carried tranquilizer pistols for situations that didn't necessitate force.

These soldiers each had high graduating scores, 98 to 100 percent in the areas of mental, physical, emotional, and sharp shooting, as well as their overall abilities to handle and assess complicated situations in real time and under pressure. They also were equipped with a modified AR-15 with extra clips.

~ ~ ~

9:32 PM

Alpha-7 was strategically placed around Amilio's compound, blending into the night. "Everything is a go, men. Close in on them," a voice said, coming over their earpieces. Right then each of the soldiers locked in the Mexican cartel goons one by one, firing off silenced rounds from their sniper rifles almost a quarter-mile away, dropping them as if they were up close and personal. Each slug traveled through the air with speed and force, splitting some of the goons in half on impact. The others' heads exploded into a pink mist.

"Jefe! The gringos are here!" he shouted, continuously spraying his AK-47 recklessly in the night, hoping the onslaught of his associates would stop. For him, it did, as a .50-caliber round pounded into his chest, thrusting him back and lifting him from his feet as it exited the other side. He was dead before his body hit the ground. Inside the mansion, Amilio was reacting fast, rounding up his men to stand guard as he was making his way to the underground tunnel he had built for moments like this. "Oye, don't let anyone come through that door! Mama!" he yelled out as she was coming down to see what's going on.

"They're coming for me, Mama. I want you to come with me. It's not safe here."

"You go, my son. I'm too old to be running. They're not going to do anything to me. When it's safe, just come back home. I'll be here."

"I want everyone in here to protect mi madre with your lives! Entiendo!"

"Si, jefe, we understand," the guard responded, making his way over to secure his mother as Amilio ran into the study where the tunnel was behind the bookcase. Once he was inside, the guard put it back as it was.

Once inside of the tunnel, Amilio hit the switch, lighting up the dark, cool, damp space. He had paid millions for this tunnel, since it led him into the United States. No one would ever expect him to run to the place he was being heavily sought. This was something he thought out years ago. He even had properties in the States he could go to, along with a few vehicles he could use at his disposal.

Close to thirty minutes after entering the tunnel, he and his guards came to a halt when he heard voices. He nodded to his men to proceed to check it out. They headed over to the split section that turned left or right, an added feature to confuse anyone chasing after him. When his men turned the corner vanishing out of his view, he heard grunting followed by a thud of bodies falling. He moved in, removing his black-pearl .40-caliber automatic. When he turned the corner, he was greeted with silenced guns aimed at him by men in black fatigues with black war paint covering their faces.

"I wouldn't do that if I were you," a voice came from behind the men in black fatigues. Amilio leaned to the side, seeing that it was Jake Rawlings of the CIA, smoking a Cohiba cigar and blowing out the smoke. "You must've forgotten that I gave you the idea for this tunnel," he said, puffing on the cigar and blowing out another cloud of smoke. "I told you this would be one of the things I miss here with you in Mexico. Then again, I came across the Diaz brothers in Sinaloa, who couldn't believe the offer I made them after you decided to continue your killing spree. That's just bad for business, my friend. So officially, I'm severing ties with you."

Before Amilio could react, the soldiers pumped multiple slugs simultaneously into his face and heart. Jake smirked, seeing a well-done performance by America's finest. "Let the rest of the Alpha-7 team know to leave no one behind. His reign and legacy all end here tonight." He tossed the cigar on Amilio's body, turning around heading home, back in control of things.

TWENTY-ONE

8:22 AM the next morning

TJ was in bed sound asleep after a long night of sex sessions. He wanted his woman to feel his love and comfort in the security he brought for her. The aroma of eggs, seasoned bacon, and scrapple with onions filled the air, waking him up. He sat up, looking out the window as the sun was shining back on him. The view of nature's landscape was pleasant to the eyes, much better than the city with blaring sirens, music, and gunshots. He slid out of bed wearing her father's pajamas with a tropical print. He clearly got them in his travels. He was making his way to the bathroom when he heard his son talking to someone besides his fiancée.

"My dad is sleeping. Are you his friends?" Hearing his son say that, TJ knew it was trouble. He ran back over to the nightstand and got his weapon before heading toward the top of the stairs. The safety was off, and one was in the chamber ready to roll. He didn't want anything to happen to his son or Lisa. He came to the large balcony that overlooked the living room area. He saw his son speaking with a Spanish female, who was in the company of a male at the door with a fully automatic B&T TP9 Uzi ready to take out a small army. He assumed they came prepared, knowing he was a trained soldier. He tried to move back, until the female looked up, noticing him as she gave off a devious smile.

"There's your dad wide awake and ready to join us," she said, now standing from the couch, displaying her Kel-Tec PLR-16 with a silencer on it. Most men would never expect a female with such beauty to be so deadly. However, this was the lifestyle she was raised in, being from Juarez. Little Tony turned to see his dad moving at the top of the steps with a gun in hand.

TJ was trying to process how he was going to take these muthafuckas. As he descended the steps, he could hear Lisa crying. When he got to the bottom of the steps, he could see why: she had a gun pointed at her head. He couldn't figure out how they tracked them.

The Mexican by Lisa took his free hand and grabbed a piece of bacon out of the pan, biting into it. "This bacon is good, like you killed the pig out back," he said, stuffing his face. "You know, technology is good for some things, but for you, my friend, it's bad, since we tracked you from that new truck. You would never think of that, but for five million, we find what we need to find," he said, unaware no one would be able to pay him since Amilio and all connected to him were killed off hours ago.

TJ was also out of the loop on this. "You came for me, so let them go. They had no part in this," TJ said, hoping no harm came to them as it had to his friends and their families.

The female present seemed as if she was in charge as she began to speak. "Your son is a cute little boy that may one day grow up into a strong man, a survivor. If he can make it through the woods alone," she said, giving him hope that she was not going to kill his son. "When I was a kid crossing the border, I traveled miles through the desert, the heat, the snakes, the scorpions and the animals that could kill a child. It sent fear through me having to fend for myself when my mother died of a heat stroke. I was eight years old, almost your son's age. I cried, but I got past my fears, and throughout the nights made my way to an old woman's house. She took me in for the night before turning me over to Immigration. I survived to come back stronger, to become who I am today. So I'm going to give your son this same chance, or you can take him with you two," she said, aiming her gun at little Tony.

"Don't kill my baby!" Lisa yelled out in fear as tears streamed down her face.

TJ was torn, not wanting to leave his son, but it was the only way he was going to make it out of here alive. He removed his dog tag. "Hey, Son, take this. I'll be with you the entire time. Listen to the flow of water, and follow it for direction to get help. If you hear people, run toward them for safety," he said, tossing the dog tag from the bottom of the steps.

Little Tony placed it around his neck, feeling some confusion, but knowing he couldn't stay. The Mexicana nodded her head to the goon at the door. He opened it, and little Tony started breathing heavily as fear came over him. As he exited the house, he turned to look at his mother. Right then the Mexican fired his gun, jolting her head as the slug forced its way through to the other side, ejecting her brains and chunks of her skull. This visual violence shook little Tony, making him take off running full speed into the woods. As he was running, another burst of bullets filled the air. He didn't look back. He could feel his feet pressing into the ground, thrusting him forward.

He ran until he heard his father's voice booming through the air calling out to him. "Tony! Tony! Come back, son, it's okay!" he said as he ran into the woods after his son. TJ reacted with lightning speed inside of the house, killing all of them once they shifted their attention on his son exiting. Then when they killed Lisa, he couldn't contain his training to kill them as fast as he could. His only regret was he couldn't save Lisa.

"Daddy!" he yelled out, running back toward the cabin.

"I'm right here, Tony!" he said, hearing the crackling of twigs he was running across. He came into view, jumping up to his father's embrace, each of them fearing what could have taken place.

"They hurt mommy," Tony said.

"I made them pay for that, Tony," TJ said, taking his son over to the truck. "Stay here." He ran into the cabin and grabbed his go bag. Then he walked over to Lisa and dropped down to her, kissing her still warm lips. "I'm sorry for this. Our son is safe now."

He raced out of the cabin into the truck and drove off. His son took the dog tag off, preparing to give it back. "No, you keep it for protection, knowing I'm with you at all times," he said, patting his son on the head, thankful he was safe. He drove for hours until he was far away and he felt it was safe. Then he got rid of the truck so he could never be tracked again.

TWENTY-TWO

2:38 PM

News of the three dead Mexican assassins traveled fast, reaching Jake Rawlings while he was at home. He saw the alert come through on his cell phone. He gave off light laughter knowing the trained soldier turned rogue cop put his skills to use to survive, which was a good trait to have. This made him an asset to Jake and the CIA, but would it be worth tracking him down at this point? Then another smirk followed by laughter came out as a thought came to him.

Meanwhile in New York at the federal correctional facility, Showtime was in his single cell watching the news of what took place in Mexico. Amilio was no more. That gave him a sense of relief. The news also displayed coverage of the aftermath at the cabin. This made him feel good seeing that his military brother got away again. As for Lisa, he felt bad for her. The reality was, now with Amilio gone, the Feds would prosecute for everything, leaving him to serve life in prison or get the death penalty. Either way, he didn't care anymore. What happened was meant to happen.

Getting his immediate attention, his door buzzed opened. With him being in a maximum-security prison on protective custody, he jumped up quick, rushing over to the door and slamming it shut. He didn't want anyone trying to get at him. As he was walking away from the door, the corridor and his cell went pitch black, followed by his cell opening again. He didn't bother shutting it this time.

He positioned himself while remaining silent, listening to other inmates yelling out about the power. Some were watching TV or listening to their radios. His door swung open, and he revved up for hand-to-hand combat, ready to fight for his life. Then all of those thoughts went out the door when he saw the red beam followed by figures moving in the darkness. "Sergeant Sean Jones?" the voice came through the air. Hearing someone address him as sergeant made him aware these men were on his side. But who were they, and who sent them? It didn't matter; they had come for him.

"Yes, that's me."

"Put these on, sir, and take this," the soldier said, blending into the dark and handing him night vision goggles with a silenced Sig Sauer Mosquito for light, quick action if needed.

They hit most of the guards with tranquilizer darts, knocking them unconscious. When they awoke they'd be long gone, and the lights would be back on. These trained men were all connected to the ring associated with the DEA they operated on the West Coast, but were under Agent Anthony, who was a mastermind. His fail-safe plan was to have either team back the other up if and when it was needed, like now. Everything hap-pened so fast, by the time they caught wind of it, they formed the group to make their way to the East Coast, but everyone was in different locations running for their lives. The men made it out of the facility down to their trucks, making their escape, driving for miles before they removed their masks.

"I want to thank all you men for not leaving me behind," Showtime said.

"You're our brother whether we served toge- ther or not. We're Marines. It's what we do. Besides, our loyalty and respects go to Agent Anthony, who made it all possible," they contin- ued, briefing him on all he needed to know before parting ways, giving him money to travel and disappear. Their job was done now. Show-time was grateful for their help. Now he had to get far and fast before they figured out he had escaped with the help of America's finest.

TWENTY-THREE

Against his better judgment, Showtime headed back to Harrisburg two days after his escape that made world news as the president expressed his thoughts on corrupt members in their government along with agents and officers. This injustice was a slap in America's face, he expressed. The president also put out an all-points bulletin on these rogue officers, making them America's most wanted.

Showtime, wearing shades and a baseball cap to downplay his look, made his way to his parents' house to see them before he vanished forever. With Amilio gone, he didn't have to fear anything or anyone.

~ ~ ~

8:44 PM

The city was dark as he moved through the alleyway heading to his parents' house on the south side of the city. He came through the backyard looking around, tuning out the barking dogs from a few houses over. He could see the light on the second floor, meaning his parents were still up. He lifted the trashcan up, retrieving the extra key before going into the house. He sat down his bag that the team gave him before they parted ways. Then he made his way through the house. As he came through the dining room, he noticed two plates with food still on them along with glasses of wine not finished. He laughed, thinking his parents may have caught the love bug in the middle of dinner. As he continued on, he saw a disruption in the furniture, the lamp tilted over, a portrait on the floor. He removed his sidearm as he proceeded with caution. He couldn't tell if all of this was recent or some time ago when they were looking for him. He started up the steps ready for the unexpected as his heart and mind raced. As he got closer to the top of the steps, he could hear the TV on, followed by his parents speaking. However, the tone in his father's voice sounded as if he was trying to reassure his mother everything was going to be okay. This made him move faster toward their bedroom. Then he heard the flushing of the toilet coming from behind him while at the same time he heard the door open.

His eyes widened in fear thinking of things going wrong as he was looking at this Mexican with a gun hanging on the strap over his shoulder. Right then he sent two rounds through the air, finding the Mexican's heart and face. In the same swift motion, he raced into his parents' room before the body hit the floor. His gun was out in front of him, taking aim and squeezing the trigger on the Latino, thrusting his body up on the dresser.

"Jesus Lord!" his mom yelled out, never seeing this type of violence up close and personal. His heart still racing, he looked on at his parents, making sure they were okay.

"I told you we're going to be okay. God takes care of us," his dad said.

"My baby boy saved us," Mrs. Jones said, extending her hand to hold her son.

"You two can't stay here. At least not for now. I want you to go over to Uncle Ronnie's house. When you get everything ready to go, call the police." He started helping them gather their things. He figured no one else should be coming.

Twenty minutes later he started heading down the steps, when he smelled smoke—smoke from a cigar. He halted his parents from coming down the stairs as he removed his gun, ready to go to protect them.

As he continued down the steps, a voice came through the air. "No need for that thing."

As he came into view, he saw a white man sitting on his parents' couch smoking a cigar.

"I don't know who you are or what you're doing in my parent's house smoking. They don't smoke, so can you put that out?"

The man looked on at Showtime as calm as

always, being in control even when things seemed out of control. "Guns kill more people than cigar or cigarette smoke. You do know that, right?" he said before introducing himself. "Jake Rawlings, I'm with the world's elite agency. Now put the gun away. If I wanted you or your parents dead, you would be already. We profiled you. We knew you would come back here, just as you saved your buddy. I am impressed with the team that assisted in your breakout. The cameras that did catch their exit shows how refined and trained they are. My team is better, but we need people of your caliber to become even better at what you trained all your life for as a Marine." He paused, allowing Showtime to take in his words. "The Mexicans weren't going to kill them. I paid them more not to. I did have a bet with the one that you would show up within three days. I win. He collects in the afterlife," he said, making himself laugh as he continued puffing his cigar.

"What about my mom and dad?"

"They're fine right where they are. I'll have people come clean up the house while they're gone."

Jake got up, making his way to the door. "You stay here and they will be coming for you, and neither you nor your friend will be able to break free from the jail they have under the desert." He exited the house at the same time Showtime hugged his parents before following Jake. "Smart move. Your talents will be used wisely instead of robbing drug dealers," he said as the truck pulled off. He puffed the cigar once more, blowing out smoke before tossing it out the window. Showtime noticed Jake wasn't alone. There were two more trucks they merged with. They headed to the airport to a private hanger with a G5 private jet that was going to take them to their destination. Showtime was now feeling the presence and power of the CIA being here. He knew with them he would no longer exist, nor would anyone be looking for him.

TWENTY-FOUR

Lincoln, Nebraska, the next day

TJ was fishing with his son enjoying life off the grid. It gave him peace of mind. The sounds of birds chirping filled the air, the sun was bright, just him and little Tony.

"Uh oh, Dad, I think I got one," little Tony said, tugging on the line reeling it in.

"You might have a big one. That's going to be

dinner," TJ joked.

"I got it, Dad," he said, struggling and taking steps backward, still reeling it in. He could see the striped bass flopping, trying to break away. "It's a big one, Dad," he said, now having it out of the water on the grass.

"You did it, Son. That's going to be fried goodness tonight."

"It sure is," a voice came from behind the two agreeing with TJ. He turned quickly and saw a tall white male looking professional. At first glance he was thinking it was the Feds. Then he scanned the area, making sure he wasn't being closed in on.

"Who are you?"

"In some cases a ghost, a nobody, but for you, I'm the guy that's going to make your life better."

"As you can see, I'm enjoying myself with my son right now, so my life is good."

"I'm sorry, let make it clear by introducing myself. Jake Rawlings, government employee. I did meet with and make Showtime the same deal I'm trying to offer you. I believe you guys have a special talent that shouldn't go to waste running for your lives or taking down drug kingpins."

TJ was now listening, wanting to make a better life for his son that didn't mean hiding or running. He, like everyone else, was aware that Showtime escaped with help from trained men. "Could these be the people that helped him?" he was thinking. "I have my son, and he needs me around right now," he said to Jake.

"We have a place for him. If need be we can set you up with a woman that knows how to be a stepmother while tending to your every desire," he said, assuring him he was going to be with the best in the world. "Just to be clear, I'm not here to negotiate. It's the best option for you right now. Otherwise, when I walk away, the Feds will know you're here and your son will be long gone."

"Okay, I'm in."

"Toss the fish back into the water and give it the second chance at life that I'm giving you," he said, making his way to the convoy of trucks. TJ just noticed them, too, as he made his way to the trucks getting in. "We have a place in Nevada that you'll train at with your team."

"I'm looking forward to it. Does this new role come with a new life, meaning no jail or people trying to kill me?"

"That's all being worked on as we speak."

Hearing this allowed him to close his eyes with his head back, relaxing until he dozed off along the three-hour ride to their location. Once they made it to the mega-complex of training facilities,

Jake led the way through each building. The first had operatives partaking in close combat with weapons. The next area was a range, followed by an area with a gym, then an area with kids playing chess, also with guns taking them apart, as well as learning how to use them.

"Your son will stay here until we're done."

"Son, are you going to be fine with these kids?" he asked, not wanting to leave him alone.

"I'll be okay, Dad. Besides, you're always with me, remember? Plus, I think I can make friends here."

TJ hugged him before heading into the next room. As soon as he entered, he saw Showtime. "I didn't think I would ever see you again," he said, embracing him like family. "Thanks for looking after me and the family."

"Anytime, brother. I'm sorry for Lisa."

"I made them pay for that shit."

Always being about business, Jake cut straight to it. "Okay, men, sorry to break up the reunion. I need you two over there with the others. Take a seat so we can get down to the important stuff," he said, referring to the team of trained men that broke Showtime out. He also had them present.

Once they were seated, six militant soldiers entered, four men and two women. Three stood on each side of them. "America is grateful for all your guys' time spent serving this country. You are the best at what you do. However, you didn't apply yourselves as you should have, which brings you all here today. The best of the best. It's truly an honor to be in your presence." Jake paused, looking to his left and his right at the men and women in gray fatigues. "Do you guys have anything to add?"

Right then each of the trained men and women in gray fatigues removed their sidearms and gunned down each of the people sitting with swift and trained precision. They didn't even see it coming or have a chance to react.

"Good work, soldiers," Jake said to the Alpha-7 team. "Sorry it had to be like this, but we do what we're told," he added, knowing these soldiers didn't favor killing their own military family. They exited the room leaving Jake to make a call. "Put me through," he said to the person on the other end of the phone. They did just that as the president came over the phone.

"I assume this call is you making America safe?"

"Yes sir, Mr. President. It's done, and I assure you this will never happen again on my watch."

"You did good, and we all appreciate you over

here."

"Thank you for giving me this opportunity," he said as the call came to an end. He was enjoying this level of power that gave him free will. He exited the room preparing to leave when little Tony noticed he was alone.

A feeling came over the nine-year-old, forcing him to react, closing in on Jake. "Excuse me, sir."

Jake turned around to the voice only to be greeted with a .380-caliber pistol staring him down. Unlike the other children in the room, little Tony already knew how to use a weapon thanks to his dad showing him. Jake stared at the kid and the gun.

"Where's my dad?" he asked, knowing he just heard gunshots, plus the six soldiers in gray exited. He knew if it was a meeting, he wouldn't be leaving so fast. Jake attempted to take the gun from the kid, to no avail. Tony pulled the trigger back-to-back, ending Jake's life with a face shot and taking away all of his power. Just like that, it was gone.

To order books, please fill out the order form below:
To order films please go to www.good2gofilms.com

Name:_____

Address:_____

City:_____State:_____Zip Code: _____

Phone:_____

Email:_____

Method of Payment: Check   VISA MASTERCARD

Credit Card#:_ _____

Name as it appears on card: _____

Signature: _____

Item Name	Price	Qty	Amount
48 Hours to Die – Silk White	$14.99		
A Hustler's Dream – Ernest Morris	$14.99		
A Hustler's Dream 2 – Ernest Morris	$14.99		
A Thug's Devotion – J. L. Rose and J. M. McMillon	$14.99		
All Eyes on Tommy Gunz – Warren Holloway	$14.99		
Black Reign – Ernest Morris	$14.99		
Bloody Mayhem Down South – Trayvon Jackson	$14.99		
Bloody Mayhem Down South 2 – Trayvon Jackson	$14.99		
Business Is Business – Silk White	$14.99		
Business Is Business 2 – Silk White	$14.99		
Business Is Business 3 – Silk White	$14.99		
Cash In Cash Out – Assa Raymond Baker	$14.99		
Cash In Cash Out 2 – Assa Raymond Baker	$14.99		
Childhood Sweethearts – Jacob Spears	$14.99		
Childhood Sweethearts 2 – Jacob Spears	$14.99		
Childhood Sweethearts 3 – Jacob Spears	$14.99		
Childhood Sweethearts 4 – Jacob Spears	$14.99		
Connected To The Plug – Dwan Marquis Williams	$14.99		
Connected To The Plug 2 – Dwan Marquis Williams	$14.99		
Connected To The Plug 3 – Dwan Williams	$14.99		
Cost of Betrayal – W.C. Holloway	$14.99		
Cost of Betrayal 2 – W.C. Holloway	$14.99		
Deadly Reunion – Ernest Morris	$14.99		
Dream's Life – Assa Raymond Baker	$14.99		
Flipping Numbers – Ernest Morris	$14.99		
Flipping Numbers 2 – Ernest Morris	$14.99		

Forbidden Pleasure – Ernest Morris	$14.99		
He Loves Me, He Loves You Not – Mychea	$14.99		
He Loves Me, He Loves You Not 2 – Mychea	$14.99		
He Loves Me, He Loves You Not 3 – Mychea	$14.99		
He Loves Me, He Loves You Not 4 – Mychea	$14.99		
He Loves Me, He Loves You Not 5 – Mychea	$14.99		
Killing Signs – Ernest Morris	$14.99		
Killing Signs 2 – Ernest Morris	$14.99		
Kings of the Block – Dwan Willams	$14.99		
Kings of the Block 2 – Dwan Willams	$14.99		
Kings of the Night	$14.99		
Lord of My Land – Jay Morrison	$14.99		
Lost and Turned Out – Ernest Morris	$14.99		
Love & Dedication – W.C. Holloway	$14.99		
Love Hates Violence – De'Wayne Maris	$14.99		
Love Hates Violence 2 – De'Wayne Maris	$14.99		
Love Hates Violence 3 – De'Wayne Maris	$14.99		
Love Hates Violence 4 – De'Wayne Maris	$14.99		
Married To Da Streets – Silk White	$14.99		
M.E.R.C. – Make Every Rep Count Health and Fitness	$14.99		
Mercenary In Love – J.L. Rose & J.L. Turner	$14.99		
Money Make Me Cum – Ernest Morris	$14.99		
My Besties – Asia Hill	$14.99		
My Besties 2 – Asia Hill	$14.99		
My Besties 3 – Asia Hill	$14.99		
My Besties 4 – Asia Hill	$14.99		
My Boyfriend's Wife – Mychea	$14.99		
My Boyfriend's Wife 2 – Mychea	$14.99		
My Brothers Envy – J. L. Rose	$14.99		
My Brothers Envy 2 – J. L. Rose	$14.99		
Naughty Housewives – Ernest Morris	$14.99		
Naughty Housewives 2 – Ernest Morris	$14.99		
Naughty Housewives 3 – Ernest Morris	$14.99		
Naughty Housewives 4 – Ernest Morris	$14.99		
Never Be The Same – Silk White	$14.99		

Scarred Faces – Assa Raymond Baker	$14.99		
Scarred Knuckles – Assa Raymond Baker	$14.99		
Secrets in the Dark – Ernest Morris	$14.99		
Shades of Revenge – Assa Raymond Baker	$14.99		
Slumped – Jason Brent	$14.99		
Someone's Gonna Get It – Mychea	$14.99		
Stranded – Silk White	$14.99		
Supreme & Justice – Ernest Morris	$14.99		
Supreme & Justice 2 – Ernest Morris	$14.99		
Supreme & Justice 3 – Ernest Morris	$14.99		
Tears of a Hustler – Silk White	$14.99		
Tears of a Hustler 2 – Silk White	$14.99		
Tears of a Hustler 3 – Silk White	$14.99		
Tears of a Hustler 4 – Silk White	$14.99		
Tears of a Hustler 5 – Silk White	$14.99		
Tears of a Hustler 6 – Silk White	$14.99		
The Betrayal Within – Ernest Morris	$14.99		
The Last Love Letter – Warren Holloway	$14.99		
The Last Love Letter 2 – Warren Holloway	$14.99		
The Panty Ripper – Reality Way	$14.99		
The Panty Ripper 3 – Reality Way	$14.99		
The Solution – Jay Morrison	$14.99		
The Teflon Queen – Silk White	$14.99		
The Teflon Queen 2 – Silk White	$14.99		
The Teflon Queen 3 – Silk White	$14.99		
The Teflon Queen 4 – Silk White	$14.99		
The Teflon Queen 5 – Silk White	$14.99		
The Teflon Queen 6 – Silk White	$14.99		
The Vacation – Silk White	$14.99		
The Webpage Murder – Ernest Morris	$14.99		
The Webpage Murder 2 – Ernest Morris	$14.99		
Tied To A Boss – J.L. Rose	$14.99		
Tied To A Boss 2 – J.L. Rose	$14.99		
Tied To A Boss 3 – J.L. Rose	$14.99		
Tied To A Boss 4 – J.L. Rose	$14.99		
Tied To A Boss 5 – J.L. Rose	$14.99		

Time Is Money – Silk White	$14.99		
Tomorrow's Not Promised – Robert Torres	$14.99		
Tomorrow's Not Promised 2 – Robert Torres	$14.99		
Two Mask One Heart – Jacob Spears and Trayvon Jackson	$14.99		
Two Mask One Heart 2 – Jacob Spears and Trayvon Jackson	$14.99		
Two Mask One Heart 3 – Jacob Spears and Trayvon Jackson	$14.99		
Wife – Assa Ray Baker & Raneissa Baker	$14.99		
Wife 2 – Assa Ray Baker & Raneissa Baker	$14.99		
Wrong Place Wrong Time – Silk White	$14.99		
Young Goonz – Reality Way	$14.99		
Subtotal:			
Tax:			
Shipping (Free) U.S. Media Mail:			
Total:			

Make Checks Payable To Good2Go Publishing, 7311 W Glass Lane, Laveen, AZ 85339